Whatever After

if the SHOE FITS

Whatever After
if the SHOE FITS

SARAH MLYNOWSKI

 Scholastic Press/New York

for my partners in crime,
lauren myracle and emily jenkins.

All rights reserved. Published by Scholastic Press, an imprint of Scholastic Inc.,
Publishers since 1920. SCHOLASTIC, SCHOLASTIC PRESS, and associated logos are
trademarks and/or registered trademarks of Scholastic Inc.

Library of Congress Cataloging-in-Publication Data

Mlynowski, Sarah.
If the shoe fits / by Sarah Mlynowski. — 1st ed.
p. cm. — (Whatever after)
Summary: On their second adventure through the magic mirror Abby and Jonah find
themselves in the Cinderella fairy tale — and that is when things start to go really wrong.
ISBN 978-0-545-41567-5
1. Cinderella (Legendary character) — Juvenile fiction. 2. Fairy tales. 3. Magic
mirrors — Juvenile fiction. 4. Brothers and sisters—Juvenile fiction. [1. Fairy
tales — Fiction. 2. Characters in literature — Fiction 3. Magic — Fiction.
4. Brothers and sisters — Fiction.] I. Title.
PZ7.M7135If 2013
813.6 — dc23
2012011967

12 11 10 9   18/0

Printed in the U.S.A.   23
First edition, January 2013

✳ chapter one ✳

My Magic Mirror Might Be Broken

I have a magic mirror in my basement and I'm going to use it.

Jonah's hand hovers in front of the mirror. "Ready?"

"Oh, yes." I am definitely ready. I've been *trying* for three days. Four nights ago, Jonah and I accidentally got sucked through the mirror and landed in Snow White's fairy tale. Well, technically, we landed in the kingdom of Zamel. Rhymes with camel. That's where Snow White lives.

If I'd known we were going to Zamel, I never would have worn slippers and pajamas. I would have worn jeans, a cute sweater, and sneakers. But I didn't even know where we were until after we'd already messed up Snow's story.

1

But don't worry! Everything ended up fine. Different, but fine.

I did leave my slippers and pajamas at Snow's, though. The slippers were pretty beaten-up anyway, but the pajamas were my favorite pair. Snow borrowed them one night and loaned me a skirt and top. Getting my pajamas back isn't the only reason I want to visit Snow. I also want to know why Maryrose, the person who lives inside our magic mirror, sent me and Jonah there in the first place. There has to be a reason, right? And why did the magic mirror in Snow's bedroom tell us not to tell our parents about what happened?

Jonah and I decided to find out.

When we'd gone to Zamel, the mirror had sucked us inside at midnight, so the night after we got home, I set my alarm for 11:51 P.M. I put on jeans. A sweater. Sneakers. I woke up my little brother, Jonah. He put on jeans. A sweatshirt. Sneakers. We crept down the two flights to the basement and closed the door behind us.

Jonah knocked. Then he knocked again. Then he knocked once more. Three times, just like the first time.

But it didn't work.

We stood there, waiting, but nothing happened.

No swirling. No hissing. No opening up its big mirror mouth and swallowing us whole.

The next night we tried again. We got up close to midnight. Put on jeans. Sweatshirts. Sneakers. Crept down to the basement. Knocked and knocked again. Knocked a third time.

Nothing, nothing, nothing!

Tonight is Night Number Three. Everyone knows three's a charm. Especially when dealing with fairy tales.

So here I am. In the basement. Again.

Jonah's fist is up against the mirror. Again.

"Ready," I say. I brace myself. Here we go. It's going to work. I know it is.

Jonah knocks.

Once.

Twice.

Three times.

No swirling, no hissing, no nothing.

I stomp my sneakered foot. "I don't get it!"

Jonah sighs in disappointment, and his skinny arm falls to his side. "Do you think it's broken?"

I peer at the antique mirror. It looks the same as it did when we first went through it. It's twice the size of me. The glass part is clear and smooth. The frame is made of stone and decorated with carvings of small fairies with wings and wands. It's attached to the wall with heavy Frankenstein bolts. We just moved to Smithville — and into our new house — a few months ago, and the mirror came with the house. I used to think the mirror was creepy. I guess it's still kind of creepy.

But it's not *just* creepy. It's also fun. It's magic.

"It doesn't look broken," I say, seeing my brother and myself in the reflection. Jonah's brown hair is short and kind of a mess, standing up in different directions. Mine is shoulder-length and wavy, but still neat. "Let me try," I add.

I knock once. Twice. Three times.

The room is still.

"Hello? Maryrose? Are you there?" I know I said Maryrose lives inside the mirror, but truthfully, I'm not sure. All I know is that Maryrose has something to do with the mirror. I think. I really don't know much. I sigh. "Maybe we imagined the whole thing."

"No way," Jonah says. "We were there. I know we were. We met Snow! We ate her stew sandwiches! Yum. I wish Mom and Dad would make them one night for dinner."

I snort. First of all, Snow's stew sandwiches were gross. And second, the likelihood of Mom and Dad trying a new recipe these days is very unlikely. Like one in a bajillion. They haven't cooked in weeks. We've ordered pizza for the last two — no, make that three — nights in a row.

Don't get me wrong, I like pizza. What ten-year-old doesn't like pizza? What adult doesn't like pizza? Jonah LOVES pizza, even though he insists on dipping the crust in ketchup, which is totally gross. But three nights in a row is extreme. What happened to cooking? What happened to meat loaf? What happened to salad?

My parents used to cook all the time, before we moved to Smithville. They had time to cook then. Now they work all the time. They're lawyers and just started their own firm. I keep telling them I'm old enough to do the cooking, but they won't listen. Just because I nearly burned down our old house when I put my socks in the toaster ONE TIME. What can I say? I wanted toasty socks. They won't even let me near the washing machine, which makes no sense. Fine. I used too much detergent and turned the laundry room into a bubble bath, but also, only ONE TIME.

I yawn. "Let's go back to bed."

"But I want an adventure! Maybe the mirror can take us to other places, too. Like Africa! Or Mars! Or Buckingham Palace!"

"We've tried three times, Jonah. We can't do this every night. We're growing kids. We need our sleep."

He twists his bottom lip. "Just one more try."

I let him try one more time even though I KNOW it's not going to work. I am three years older than he is. I know these things. And I'm right. Of course I'm right. I'm always right. I march him up the stairs, back up to the top floor, and steer him toward his room.

He kicks off his sneakers and plants his face on his bed.

Back in my room, as I change back into my second-favorite pair of pajamas, I can't help but wonder if we really did imagine the whole thing.

But wait! My jewelry box is sitting on my dresser, and on the lid of my jewelry box are illustrations of fairy tale characters. Snow White is right between Cinderella and the Little Mermaid. Snow is definitely not wearing her puffy dress. She's wearing my lime-green pajamas, which means it really *did* happen.

So why isn't the mirror working?

* chapter two *

No More Cereal, Please

blah, grumble, blah.

Yes, I'm cranky this morning. Why?

1. I'm tired from last night.
2. I'm having cereal for breakfast AGAIN when there is a full carton of eggs in the fridge.
3. I have nothing to wear because all my clothes are dirty.

It's not like I need a hot breakfast all the time, but the eggs are going bad TOMORROW. I know because I checked the carton.

7

Are my parents ever going to cook them? Why did they bother buying them?

And the laundry! They haven't done the laundry in more than a week! What is up with that?

"I am down to my monkey underwear," I say, shifting uncomfortably. My mother should know what this means. I have two pairs of monkey undies and I never, ever, EVER wear them unless I absolutely have to, since I am not a fan of wedgies. I should have just thrown them out. Of course, if I had thrown them out, then I'd have to go to school wearing dirty undies. Yuck. What I really need is for a) my parents to take me shopping, or b) for them to do laundry, but it's not like either will happen, since they barely have time to brush their teeth.

Seriously, I think my dad forgot to brush his teeth this morning. His breath smells like last night's pepperoni.

My mom ruffles my hair. "Sorry, honey. I'll try to get to the laundry tonight."

"If I run out of laundry, can I wear my Spider-Man bathing suit under my jeans?" Jonah asks.

"No, sweetie," Dad says. "You wouldn't be comfortable."

Like wedgies are comfortable?

It's the end of the day and I'm in bed and I'm not happy.

1. We had pizza for dinner. Again. Forget smelling like
   a pepperoni. I might turn *into* a pepperoni.
2. No one did the laundry tonight. I will have to wear
   my second pair of monkey underwear tomorrow,
   which means I will have a wedgie *again*. And after
   that — shudder, shudder — it's dirty undies for me.

Jonah, who is supposed to be asleep since his bedtime was an
hour ago, pops his head into my doorway and whispers, "See
you at midnight!"

I purse my lips. "Fine. I'll try again, but it's not like I expect
it to work."

"I bet it does!" he cheers.

"And what are you basing that on? The fact that it hasn't
worked for the past three days?" I ask in my best lawyer voice.
I'm going to be a lawyer when I grow up. Not because I want to
be a lawyer, but because I want to be a judge. You have to be a

lawyer before you can be a judge. That's the rule. For the record, when I'm a lawyer, I'm still going to do stuff like laundry and cook.

"It has to work at some point," Jonah reasons. "I'm setting my alarm."

I flump my head back on my pillow. "Fine. So will I."

I will humor my brother and return to the basement. But this is the last time. After tonight the mirror is dead to me. Enough is enough.

"Abby! Wake up! Let's go."

I open one eye, then the other. Doesn't my brother know that he's supposed to knock? That's the rule.

My alarm rings and I reach out to turn it off. Grumble. So. Not. In. The. Mood. But I swing my legs over the side of the bed anyway.

"Aren't you changing?" Jonah asks. He's wearing jeans. A red sweatshirt. Sneakers.

"Nope." I am staying in my pink pajamas with purple polka dots. Not anything I'd ever be caught in outside my house, but I'm not worried. It's not like the mirror's going to work.

Okay, here's the secret thing. Have you ever heard the expression "A watched pot never boils"? My nana says it all the time. It means if you're waiting for something to happen, it won't. But if you don't wait, it will. Like when you're waiting for your friend to call you back and you stare at the phone, hoping it will ring. It doesn't. But if you go off and do your homework, before you know it, your friend calls and — yay! — interrupts you.

So here's what I'm thinking: What if *this* is like *that*? When I get all dressed up expecting the mirror to let me in, it doesn't work. But if I wear the most RIDICULOUS pajamas I have, the only ones that happen to be clean, then the mirror will think I'm not expecting it and will finally let us in!

I shove the thought back down deep inside my brain. If the mirror knows I'm trying to trick it, then my trick isn't going to work.

La, la, la. No tricks here. Just wearing my ridiculous pajamas.

And sneakers. (No choice. The basement floor is cold, and my slippers are still at Snow's.)

I climb down the stairs with Jonah. I close the basement door. We stand in front of the mirror.

Jonah knocks once.

He knocks twice.

"Ready?" he asks.

"Whatever," I say, trying to sound bored.

He knocks a third time — thrice.

Ha, isn't that a funny word? It sounds like a kitchen utensil. To make the eggs really fluffy, I need to use the thrice. Except no one in my house eats eggs anymore.

"Abby —"

"It didn't work," I say. "Let's go back to bed. I'm tired."

"But, Abby —"

"Maybe we *did* just imagine the whole thing. Even the jewelry box. Or maybe Maryrose left town. Maybe she came with us to Snow's story and stayed there. Maybe —"

"Abby!"

"What?"

Jonah is pointing at the mirror. "Look!"

I look. It's spinning. It's hissing. It's turning purple. It's working?

Oh. My. Goodness. It's working!

"Wahoo!" Jonah cheers. "We're going back in!"

We're going back in! We're going back in! We're going back in and I'm wearing polka-dot pajamas.

✳ chapter three ✳

This Is Not a Forest

*J*onah jumps on his toes. "Let's just step inside before it eats us."

"Good idea," I say. "Maybe then it won't gobble up any more furniture." Last time, the mirror sucked up a swivel chair and most of my parents' old law books. I guess the plus side of our parents being too busy for even teeth brushing is they haven't come down here in the last few days. They'd have a million questions and I'd have no answers.

"I can't wait to see Snow!" Jonah exclaims. "And the dwarfs! And everyone!"

I grab my brother's hand. "Me too. Let's do it!"

We hold tight and walk in. At first it feels like we're stepping into a vacuum cleaner. I close my eyes. Then, *thump*.

I land on my butt and open my eyes. I expect to smell trees. Or ground. Last time, we arrived in the middle of a forest.

We are not in a forest.

Where are we? All I see is white. And NOT as in Snow White. "Jonah? You okay?"

"I'm tangled."

"In what?" I have no idea where I am. Why do I only see white? Am I in a marshmallow? I reach out to touch the whiteness. It's furry.

It's an animal. Crumbs! An animal ate me! "Help!" I scream. "I've been eaten!"

I try to push myself to safety. I end up petting it. Aw. So soft!

It doesn't move. I push the furry thing off me and stand up. The fur is on a coat hanger. "Oh! It's a coat!"

I glance around the small space. We're surrounded by coats. Wait a sec. "We're in a coatroom!"

There are about a hundred coats all around. Leather coats. Wool coats. Mink coats. Hats. Shoes. Ponchos.

"Are we at the dry cleaner's?" Jonah asks.

"It's a closet. A coat closet, I think," I say. The door to the closet is slightly ajar, and a stream of candlelight is shining in.

"I don't remember Snow having a closet like this," Jonah says.

"No. Hmm. What's that sound? Do you hear music?"

Jonah nods. There are trumpets and some drums. Dance music. Is it a party?

The closet door swings open. Holding a green cloth coat, a skinny young man with a goatee and wearing a purple uniform grabs a hanger off the pole.

I try to duck, but it's too late.

"What are you doing in here?" he screeches.

"We're not sure?" I say like it's a question.

"You kids better not be stealing coats!" he yells. "I'm up for a promotion and I can't get fired!"

"We're not, we swear," I hurry to say.

"We're here to see Snow," Jonah adds.

The guy blinks. "It's snowing? I should salt the stairs."

"Not snow, the weather," Jonah explains. "Snow, the person."

The guy shakes his head. "Snow is a name?"

"Yes!" I say. "She's the queen!" Who *is* this guy?

He hangs up the green cloth coat. "Clarissa is the queen of Floom."

"Floom?" I repeat.

"Yes, Floom."

"We're in Zamel," I say.

"No," the skinny guy says, tugging on his goatee. "Floom."

"Rhymes with room," Jonah says.

"And loom," the guy says. He eyes us suspiciously. "You're not from here, are you?"

"We're from Smithville," I say.

"Is that far?" he asks.

"About a mirror away," I mumble. "So there's definitely no Snow White here? I wonder where we are. Another story maybe. You said the queen is Clarissa?"

"And the king is Eugene, and the prince is Jordan."

"Is there a princess?" I ask.

"Not yet. Of course we're all hoping that will change. How old are you, nine?"

"Ten and a half, thank you very much." Humph. I try to push past him, but he blocks my way.

"What are you doing here?" he asks. He looks me over. "Are you the court jester?"

My cheeks burn. "No, I am not!" I really did not think this pajama-wearing plan through.

"Well, you're too young to be eligible for marriage."

"Um, no kidding."

A man and a woman, both wearing sheepskin coats, approach the coat man. "Don't go anywhere," the coat man says to us. "I have to help them."

Right. And where would we go? We're stuck in a closet.

He bows to the couple. The guy is wearing a tuxedo and she's in a long satin dress.

We *are* at a party. A fancy party.

"Oh my gosh, we're at a fancy party and I'm wearing pajamas!" I exclaim to Jonah. "How embarrassing. Maybe I should just stay in the closet."

"Do you think it's a wedding?" Jonah asks.

"Maybe."

"A swect sixteen."

"Could be."

"A bat mitzvah?"

"I don't know, Jonah." I'm going to have a bat mitzvah when I'm twelve. There's no way it will be this fancy, though.

I peek at the woman as her escort hands her coat to the coat guy.

Speaking of fancy — her dress is covered in shiny beads and sequins, and has a huge poofy skirt.

She's wearing a ball gown. Which makes this a ball.

A ball. We're at a ball. My head nearly explodes. "Jonah! Look at her dress! Do you know what this means?"

"You're really, really underdressed?"

I wave my hand. "You're hardly wearing a tuxedo. But besides that. We're at a ball. Think. Who has a ball?"

"I have a soccer ball. I think it's somewhere in the back-yard, but I —"

"Not that kind of ball, Jonah. A *ball* ball. A party ball. We went through the mirror, but we're not in Snow White's story. We're at a ball and there's a prince. A prince looking for his prin-cess. We're in —"

His eyes light up. "Africa? Mars? Buckingham Palace?"

I smile. "No, Jonah. *Cinderella*."

✴ chapter four ✴

Hello, Ball

d o you know Cinderella?" I ask the coat guy.

He scratches his goatee. "Never heard of her."

"Maybe you're wrong. Maybe we're not in Cinderella's story," Jonah says.

"No, no, we are," I say, thinking fast. "The coat man works in the palace, which means he probably doesn't know Cinderella. Her family hides her away in the house!"

"If you say so." Jonah pauses. "Can we go explore?"

Jonah always wants to explore. Floom. Zamel. The basement.

"Wait a second," the coat guy says before Jonah can drag me away. "Are you supposed to be here? Were you invited?"

"Not exactly —" Jonah begins.

I shoot him a look. If the coat guy kicks us out, we're in big trouble. The mirror that will take us home is probably here in the palace. Also, I want to see Cinderella. What girl doesn't love Cinderella? That awesome dress! The glass slippers!

I've always wanted a pair of glass slippers. Also ruby slippers. Hmm, I wonder why we call the glass slippers *slippers*? They're not slippers. They're high heels.

The coat man is staring at me. Oh, right. I need to come up with a reason why we're here. "We're um . . . looking for our parents!" I say. "They brought us here and told us to hang out while they talked to their friends."

Okay, fine. So I stretched the truth a bit.

A lot, actually. But desperate times call for desperate measures. We just got here. We can't get in trouble already!

The coat guy frowns. "Well, I suppose the king will enjoy your outfit."

Humph. I guess he's being sarcastic.

He narrows his eyes. "You're sure your parents are here?"

Jonah and I both nod.

The coat guy shrugs. "All right. Go ahead. Have fun."

We step out of the closet. We're standing in some sort of

entranceway. The ceilings in this place are really high. Soaring. It reminds me of my school gym. Except it's much, much nicer. And less smelly.

"Look," Jonah says. "There's a painting on the ceiling!"

I look up. It's a painting of people. Royal people. Hundreds of royal people. I can tell they're royal because they're all wearing crowns. I guess this royal family has been around for a long time. I feel eyes on me and look back down. The man and the woman who just checked their coats are staring at me.

Or, more likely, staring at my pajamas.

How rude. This can't be their first time they ever saw pajamas. They don't have to *stare*.

"Let's go inside the ballroom," Jonah says excitedly.

I notice an elderly woman eyeing me, too.

"But people are looking at me," I whisper.

"So?" Jonah asks.

"They think I'm weird!"

"You are! Who cares? Let's go to the party!"

"But I'm too obvious in my pajamas! And you, too! You're wearing a red sweatshirt and jeans. Do you see anyone else wearing a sweatshirt and jeans? We're at a ball!"

"No one is noticing me with you in that outfit, trust me."

"Thanks," I retort. "We have to be careful. What if someone says something to the prince? What if Cinderella sees me? What if I mess up the whole story?"

Jonah ignores me. "Do you think they have snacks? I bet they have dogs-in-a-blanket. It seems like the kind of party that has dogs-in-blankets."

"Do you mean those mini–hot dogs? They're called pigs-in-a-blanket."

"No, they're not." He adamantly shakes his head. "Why would they be called pigs-in-a-blanket when they're *hot dogs*? They're not *hot pigs*."

"I didn't make this up, Jonah. I'm just correcting you."

"Who cares what they're called? I just want to eat them. Let's go!" Instead of waiting for me to respond or grant him permission, he takes off.

Why doesn't he realize that I am the older sibling and therefore responsible for making all the decisions?

I run after him into the ballroom.

Wow. There are, like, a thousand people here. No wonder Cinderella was upset that she wasn't invited.

"Look," I say, pointing. Up on a stage are two people sitting on two purple thrones. "They must be the king and queen."

The queen is smiling a perfect smile. Her teeth are the color of white chalk, and she has long wavy blond hair. She looks like a real-life Barbie. Or maybe a beauty pageant contestant.

The king is sitting next to her, looking bored. He keeps yawning.

Between him and his wife is a humongous flag.

The Floom flag, probably. The design? Pink with purple polka dots.

I look down at my pajamas. I look back at the flag.

I look down again. I look back up.

I look around and see that a crowd of people are waving and smiling at me. "Great outfit!" one woman cheers.

Oh my goodness! No wonder no one has kicked me out. I am wearing the Floom flag! I'm their mascot.

I'm going to blend right in!

Wait. Maybe that's why the mirror finally let us through. Yes! We never would have been accepted here if I wasn't wearing this Floom flag pair of pajamas.

Our magic mirror sure is smart.

Out of the corner of my eye, I spot the prince.

I can tell he's the prince because:

1. He's handsome.
2. He's youngish (like an older teenager).
3. He's wearing some sort of royal purple robe. (Or maybe it's just a bathrobe over *his* pj's, but I highly doubt it.)
4. He's wearing a crown.
5. He's surrounded by a ton of girls. There are many giggles and a lot of hair flipping. It's like watching one of those dating reality shows that my mom used to watch when she had time for TV. The girls look so silly. I'm *so* embarrassed for them.

"Princes wear crowns, too?" Jonah asks. "Can I wear a crown?"

I snort. "Are you a prince?"

"Mom says I'm *her* prince."

"Then ask Mom to get you a crown. Maybe she'll make you one out of tinfoil."

"Never mind," he says. "It looks kind of heavy. Hey, is that Cinderella?" he asks, pointing to the girl standing next to the prince.

"Her? No way." The girl he's pointing to is wearing a beige dress with a gold choker around her neck. She's definitely not Cinderella.

"How do you know?" Jonah asks.

"Because . . . because . . ." Her hair isn't straight and it's not curly. It's more zig-zaggy. A little frizzy.

And it's not blond. Or brunette. It's in the middle.

And her eyes aren't blue or green or sparkly. They're small. And her lips are kind of thin. "She's average-looking," I answer. She's not ugly or anything — she's just ordinary. Plain. And Cinderella is supposed to be the MOST beautiful girl in all the land.

"Are you sure?" Jonah asks. "The prince is talking to her. He seems to like her. Isn't that how the story goes?"

I look more closely and have to agree. The prince *is* talking to her. He's even laughing at something she's saying. But it doesn't mean he wants to marry her, does it? I mean, I laughed when Zach Rothenberg stuffed an edamame up his nose in the school cafeteria, but it doesn't mean I want to marry *him*.

25

There's a sudden trumpet sound at the door. Everyone in the room turns to look.

Then one of the doormen announces, "The gorgeous stranger princess has arrived!"

The gorgeous stranger princess?

Cinderella!

✳ chapter five ✳

There She Is, Miss America. Oops. Miss Floom.

I study the prince to see how he reacts. First, he turns to look at his dad, the king, who motions to the door. I'm guessing that's his royal order to Go Get the Stranger Princess. The prince nods and makes his way outside.

And the girl he was talking to? Her face falls. Aw. I can't help but feel bad for her. But come on! How can a regular girl compete with Cinderella?

Cinderella! I'm going to see Cinderella!

The entire crowd drifts out the door to see.

Oh. My. Goodness.

First we see a gold coach. "That used to be a pumpkin!" I whisper to Jonah.

Then I motion to the six gray neighing horses. "Those were mice!"

Standing by the coach are six footmen and a plump coachman.

"What were those?" Jonah asks.

"The coachman was a rat, I think. But I forget what the footmen were. Spiders? No, lizards, maybe?"

Here she comes! First her foot. Her glass-slippered foot. The crowd oohs and aahs.

She steps out of the coach just like a movie star at a Hollywood premiere.

Everyone gasps.

I gasp. She really is gorgeous.

Her dress is gorgeous, too.

She looks just like she does on my jewelry box, in her ball gown. She's so sophisticated. So stunning. So sparkly!

"She's breathtaking," a young man with thick black glasses says.

"But who is she?" a woman with bright pink lipstick asks. "Is she really a princess?"

"She's not from around here, that's for sure," an older woman leaning against a cane says, then clucks her tongue. "Trust me. I would know. I know everyone."

"Her dress is real silver!" pink-lipstick woman says.

"No, it's platinum," the older woman declares. "That's better than silver. It's even better than gold. Trust me."

The dress glitters. Cinderella glitters. Her blond hair is pulled up and back in some sort of super-awesome knot, and her face is made up. Red lipstick. Blush. Silver eye shadow.

Or maybe it's platinum.

You can see her blue eyes even from here. They're practically glowing.

The prince appears beside her. "Hello," he says gallantly. "Nice to see you again."

"Hi," she responds, batting her mascaraed eyelashes. "It's nice to see you again, too."

Huh? Again?

"I don't get it," Jonah says. "He knows her already?"

That is weird. How does he already know her? I tap the cane woman on the shoulder. "Excuse me," I ask. "How does the prince know Cinder — I mean, the beautiful stranger princess?"

She rolls her eyes. "They met at the first ball."

Oh! Right! There were a whole bunch of versions of *Cinderella*, and some of them had more than one ball. My nana is a literature professor and she used to read all the original fairy tales to me when we lived near her in Naperville.

I just don't remember how many balls there were. Hmm. Probably three. Of course — everything in fairy tales happens in threes.

"So there are three balls?" I ask.

She clucks her tongue. "*Noooo.* Two. Yesterday's and today's. That's it."

I guess not *everything* happens in threes. I turn back to Cinderella. She looks so beautiful. He looks so handsome. They are a perfect fairy tale couple. "Isn't it romantic?" I swoon. "Isn't it wonderful?"

"The other girl doesn't think it's so wonderful," Jonah comments, pointing with his chin toward the girl who was talking to the prince before he dumped her for Cinderella.

The average-looking girl.

She does look kind of devastated. I don't blame her — she was making the prince laugh before Cinderella showed up. If she would have asked me, I would have told her to back off — she was asking for heartbreak.

Really, everyone should consult me before making decisions. It's for their own good.

"Abby, what now?" Jonah asks.

"One sec," I say. I can't help but follow Cinderella and the prince as they walk back into the ballroom. They're magnetic. All the guests point and gasp. Even the music stops.

Everyone's mesmerized. Everyone except my brother, but he's a seven-year-old boy. He can't be expected to appreciate epic romance.

The prince wraps his arm around Cinderella's waist and takes her hand.

Sigh.

The music restarts. My heart soars. They begin to dance.

Rumors and whispers swirl.

"I heard she's the heiress to a diamond dynasty!"

"I heard she's the youngest princess in Roctavia!"

"I heard she's turned down thirteen marriage proposals, but thinks our prince is the one!"

I cover my mouth so I don't laugh.

"Abby," Jonah whispers. "They're wrong, right? Isn't she just an ordinary girl whose fairy godmother made her look pretty to come to the ball?"

"She was always pretty," I say. "But her mom died and then —"

"How come the mother always dies in fairy tales? Snow White's mom died, too."

"I don't know, Jonah. I don't write these things, I just read them. Where was I?"

"Dead mother."

"Right. Her mom died and her dad remarried an evil stepmother."

"Again with the evil stepmother!"

"Tell me about it."

"But the evil stepmother had daughters?"

"Yes. Two. And they're not as beautiful as Cinderella."

"And why is she at the ball again?"

Luckily I paid attention to Nana's stories 100 percent of the time. Jonah, about 30 percent.

"The stepmom was invited. She was planning to go with her stepdaughters, hoping that the prince would fall in love with one of them and make her a princess. Cinderella wanted to go, too, but her stepmom said no way. She made her sleep in the attic and do all the housework. Cinderella cried, and then presto, up popped her fairy godmother who said she was going to help her. She turned a bunch of animals into the coach and footmen, and her rags into a beautiful dress. She gave Cinderella glass slippers. She's an awesome stylist, this fairy godmother. Wish I had one. Anyway, she told Cinderella to leave the ball by midnight."

"Why?"

"Because that's when all the magic ends."

"But if she's a fairy godmother, why can't she make it last longer?"

I shrug. "I don't know. But what happens next — what happens now — is that Cinderella's having so much fun that she nearly forgets it's midnight. She runs and drops her shoe —"

"I thought there were two balls?" Jonah asks.

"Oh. Right. I don't remember every single detail, but I think at the first ball Cinderella danced with the prince but then remembered to leave before midnight. But the final ball is when she loses track of time and then drops her shoe. Her dress turns back into rags, and the coachmen and the footmen and the coach turn back to mice and rats and lizards and a pumpkin. Meanwhile, the prince picks up the shoe and promises that whoever the shoe fits will be his wife. Over the next few days, his assistant goes around to all the households in the kingdom and makes the ladies try on the slipper. It fits Cinderella perfectly. She shows him the second shoe as proof and all is well. She gets married to the prince and is rescued from her mean stepmother. And they live happily ever after." Sigh. I love this story.

"What happens to the stepsisters?"

"In the classic version, I think it was written by some French guy, Perrault or Poutine or something, Cinderella forgives them. That's the one Nana liked the best. In the others I think it's kinda grosser."

His eyes light up. "Tell me!"

My brother loves the gross parts.

"Well, in the Grimm brothers' one, the stepsisters try to cut off their heels and toes to fit into the slipper. And then they die."

"No way! Awesome!"

I roll my eyes.

"Snack?" a waiter interrupts us, waving a plate in front of us.

"Dogs-in-a-blanket!" Jonah cheers.

I roll my eyes again. But I take two.

Jonah takes three and stuffs them all in his mouth. "So what do we do now? Explore?"

"Can you swallow before talking, please? Where are your manners? We're at a ball."

"Why should I listen to you? You're wearing pink pajamas with purple polka dots."

Humph. "I think we should find the magic mirror that will take us home first so we're not rushing around later."

"Then we can explore?"

"Yeah. But let's start with the mirror. It's probably somewhere in the castle. Looking for it is exploring, right? Now's our best chance anyway since the royal family and the staff are distracted by the ball. But we have to be careful not to get in Cinderella's way. We can't risk messing up the story!"

He wiggles his eyebrows. "You don't want to say hi? Even quickly?"

"Of course I do, but we can't. We learned our lesson with Snow White. We will NOT mess the story up this time around!" No way, no how, no thank you.

* chapter six *

Mirror, Mirror, Let Me In

We find twelve mirrors in the castle:

The mirror in the queen's room. The king's room. The prince's room. The guest rooms. The maids' rooms. There are even two in the ballroom.

None of them work.

And knocking on them isn't always easy, either.

There was a maid in the queen's room. We told her that Her Majesty requested her presence downstairs so that we could continue "exploring."

If we don't stop exploring soon, we are definitely going to get caught.

"Now what? We've tried all of them!" Jonah huffs after we've visited every room — thrice.

"Maybe the magic mirror isn't at the palace," I say. "Maybe it's at Cinderella's house. Snow White lived in the palace before she had to run away. So maybe the portal is where the main character originally lives, before she gets to live happily ever after."

"But we don't even know where Cinderella lives!"

"We can follow her home," I say. "*She* knows where she lives."

"Do you think she's still here?" Jonah asks.

"Wait, what time is it?" I glance down at my watch. Oh, no! I'm not wearing my watch! I took it off last night before bed. Not that my watch would tell me what time it is here. But it would tell me what time it is at home so we could get home before my parents wake up. And now I have no idea what time it is in Smithville!

ARGH.

Jonah follows me sneakily down the hallway back into the ballroom, and I spot a huge round clock hanging on the far wall.

It's 11:55.

I scan the room for Cinderella and spot her dancing with the prince.

Now the clock says 11:56. Hmm. Does Cinderella not realize what time it is?

"It's getting late," Jonah says. "We should tell her to go. Doesn't she turn into a pumpkin at twelve?"

"Her coach turns into a pumpkin, not her." I grab hold of his sleeve. "But no, don't do anything! We don't want to mess anything up."

We wait. We watch. 11:58. 11:59.

My heart thumps. What if our just being here messed things up? What if we don't have to do anything but be here and the story changes anyway? What if she changes back into her rags right here and everyone gasps and freaks out and the prince doesn't want to marry her after all?

Twelve!

Ding Dong! Ding Dong! Ding Dong!

Cinderella looks up at the clock. Her face pales when she sees the time. She looks at the prince, says good-bye, and then — sprints!

Like really fast!

She makes a mad dash right out of there.

She doesn't look back, she just goes, goes, GOES!

Zoom! Rhymes with Floom!

"We have to follow her," I order Jonah, and sprint right behind her. "If we lose her, we won't know where she lives!"

"At least we didn't mess up the story," Jonah calls out.

We follow her outside. She's running down the steps of the palace, and the prince is chasing after her. She's in the front, Jonah and I are to her left, and the prince is behind us. We're a triangle on the move.

On the bottom step, her glass slipper falls off, just like it's supposed to. Yes! We didn't mess anything up!

She glances back for a second, but sees the prince behind her and doesn't stop moving.

She just goes, goes, GOES!

"Wait! Wait! WAIT!" the prince yells.

I look behind and see that he's stopped. He bends down and picks up the slipper.

Jonah and I, however, keep on running.

Cinderella jumps into her coach and shouts, "Go, go, GO!"

The footmen and horses go, go, GO!

"Oh, no!" Jonah exclaims. "How are we going to keep up on foot?"

"Run," I order. "Fast, fast, FAST!"

We chase the coach down the block. I'm huffing and puffing, and I really need to do more exercise because I am not in very good shape and —

I see a spark up ahead. Like someone is lighting a match.

The coach begins to glimmer. The horses are shaking. Something is happening.

Kabam!

The coach is shrinking! The horses are shrinking! The footmen are shrinking!

Poof!

Cinderella is sitting on her butt in the middle of the street next to a squashed pumpkin.

The horses are mice. The footmen are lizards. The coachman is a rat.

The whole transformation only took about two seconds. I wish I had my dad's video camera so I could put it on YouTube.

Jonah is standing beside me with his jaw wide open. "Did anyone else see that? Someone else must have seen that!"

I look around the empty moonlit street. We're the only witnesses.

"Oh well," Cinderella says to herself. She looks nothing like the Cinderella of two minutes ago. No wonder her own family didn't recognize her. Her hair hangs around her shoulders, and she's no longer wearing any platinum eye shadow or red lipstick or any makeup at all. Her dress is plain brown. Her jewelry is gone, too. She stands up and brushes her dress off. She takes off her right glass slipper and starts walking barefoot.

"What do we do now?" Jonah asks.

Isn't it obvious? "We follow her home."

✳ chapter seven ✳

Just Pretend You Don't See Us

We follow her for the next thirty minutes, all the way to her house. It's a good thing there's a full moon because this town doesn't have any streetlights.

We keep a safe distance. We only whisper. We duck into the shadows whenever Cinderella turns around. We're really good at this sneaky thing. I bet we could be spies when we grow up. We'd be the cool brother-and-sister team that gets to go to exotic places like New York or Japan to steal nuclear power secrets. They'll make a movie about us! It'll be called —

"WHY ARE YOU PEOPLE FOLLOWING ME?"

Oops.

Cinderella is glaring at us from her porch, her hands on her hips.

"We're not following you," I squeak.

"Um, yes you are. You followed me all the way from the palace."

"No, we —" I stop in mid-sentence. We *are* following her. I'm not sure what to say.

"We need to use your house," Jonah says.

"There's a public bathroom three blocks over," Cinderella says.

"No, so we can go home," I say.

"What? Who are you?"

"I'm Abby, and this is my brother, Jonah."

"Don't you have your own house?" she asks.

"We do, but we need to use yours to get back to it."

"I don't understand," she says. "Anyway, I can't let you in. My stepmother is really strict, and if I don't listen to her, I get into trouble."

"Your stepmother is still at the ball," I say. "We'll be in and out before she gets home."

"Yeah," Jonah pipes up, "but even if you did get into trouble, it won't be for long 'cause you're going to marry the prince!"

Her eyes widen. "Excuse me?"

Uh-oh. "Jonah, no!"

Jonah turns to me, cheeks reddening. "What? Was I not supposed to tell her?"

Cinderella steps down from the porch. "Why would you say I was going to marry the prince?"

"I don't see what the big deal is," Jonah says to me. "Why shouldn't she know her future?" He grins at Cinderella. "You were at the ball, right? You danced with the prince and he thinks you're the prettiest girl around. You're going to get married."

"But — but I don't understand!" she sputters. "How would he find me? He'll never recognize me! Even my own stepmother and stepsisters didn't recognize me!"

I sigh. Since the cat is out of the bag, I guess there's no reason to keep it all a secret. "You dropped your shoe, right? He picked it up. Tomorrow he's going to make an announcement that he's going to marry the person who fits the shoe. He sends his assistant to make every girl in the kingdom try it on. It only fits you."

A slow smile spreads across Cinderella's face. "Seriously?"

"Seriously," I say. "You're going to be a princess — and then you'll get married and be his queen. Well, at first you'll just be a princess, but eventually you'll get to be queen once his dad . . .

you know." No need to be morbid. "Anyway, my point is that even if your stepmother is ticked off at you for a few days, it won't matter in the long run."

"Squee!" Cinderella squeals. "That is absolutely the best news ever. I can't believe the prince picked up my slipper!"

"It was lucky," I say. It probably would have been luckier if the prince had caught up with her, but who am I to judge?

One day I'll be a judge. But not yet.

"It's also lucky that it only fits you," Jonah says.

"They're perfectly molded to my feet." She lifts the remaining shoe so that it's eye level. "See?"

And there it is. Right in front of me. The infamous glass slipper. "Can I hold it?" I ask breathlessly.

"Sure," she says, and passes it to me.

Whoa. It's heavier than I thought. And it's really made of glass. Completely see-through. It feels like I'm holding one of my parents' for-company-only wineglasses. But it's a shoe. A really high-heeled shoe. I'm not sure how she even walked in them. And they're tiny, too. For an adult. Or an almost-adult, anyway — I'm guessing she's about sixteen. The weird thing about the shoe? There are toe marks where the toes go. This shoe was perfectly molded to fit Cinderella's foot. I guess that makes sense for the story — if they were just a size five, then other girls with size-five feet could fit in them, too.

I hand it back. I really don't want to drop it by accident.

"Why didn't the glass slipper disappear like the rest of the stuff?" Jonah asks.

"My fairy godmother changed the dress and coach and horses from something else," Cinderella explains. "But she gave me the shoes as a gift. The slippers are made just for me, you know."

"High heels," I say.

"What?"

I wave my hand. Never mind.

"Anyway, how do you know what's going to happen to me?" Cinderella asks. "Are you some type of fairy?"

"No," Jonah says. "But we're in a fairy tale."

She scrunches her nose. "Does that mean a fairy told you what happens to me?"

"Well . . . kind of," I say. A fairy *tale* told us what happened. Close enough. "Can we come in? We don't have much time. We need to get moving before your family gets home."

"All right," Cinderella says, and unlocks the door.

We step into a fancy foyer. Not as fancy as the palace, but still fancy. The tiles on the floor are checkerboard, black and white. There's a big couch, a love seat, chairs, a fireplace, and a wood grandfather clock up against the wall.

There's a lit chandelier above us, and a big rectangular mirror right by the entranceway.

"Let's try it," I say. "Cinderella, stand back. We definitely can't take you home with us. That would mess up your life for sure."

Jonah knocks. Once. Twice. Thrice! Nothing.

Boo. "How many other mirrors do you have in the house?"

"My stepmother has one in her room, and my stepsisters have two. That's it. But why do you need to use a mirror to get home? Where do you live? I don't understand."

"Neither do we," I say. "But that's the way the magic works. Why do we need a mirror to get home? Why did you have to leave the ball by midnight?"

"Magic is weird," she says. "Let's go."

On the second floor, there are two rooms and another staircase.

"Where's your room?" I ask Cinderella.

She points up. "The attic. Let's start in my stepmother's room." She throws the door open and motions to the large mirror by her bed.

I knock. Once. Twice. Thrice!

Nothing.

"Argh!" I say.

There's a noise outside. It's a carriage.

"Look who it is," Cinderella says with a smirk. "My step-mother and stepsisters returning from the ball. Wait until I tell them what you told me."

My mouth goes dry. "No, no, no. You can't say anything to them!"

"Why not? You said it's going to happen! Were you not telling me the truth?"

"I was telling you the truth, but who knows what will happen if you say something? What if they try to stop it? What if they mess something up? You have to keep it a secret! Promise me you'll keep it a secret!"

"Okay, okay," she grumbles. "If you think I have to."

"*We* have to hurry," Jonah says. "We don't want them to see us, right?"

"Let's go. To the stepsisters' room! One of those mirrors had better work."

"Abby, what if they don't? How will we get home?"

"I don't know!"

Last chance. Here we go.

* chapter eight *

Double Trouble

I can see in the moonlight that the room is all pink. Two pink beds, two pink carpets, two pink desks, two pink wardrobes, and two pink pillows — one embroidered with the name *Kayla*, the other with the name *Beatrice*.

But best of all: two full-sized pink-framed mirrors.

I have a good feeling about these mirrors, I really do.

Jonah runs straight to Kayla's mirror. "Maybe they both work. We each get our own portal, how cool is that?"

"Do you really think I'd let you walk into a mirror by yourself?" I say. "What if you actually end up on Mars or something? Not happening. Let's just choose one and go for it."

Cinderella is looking out the window. "Hurry! They're getting out of the coach! They won't like this one bit! Last month they caught me napping in here and they locked me in their closet for two hours!"

I shiver. They sound awful. I take Jonah's hand and knock. "One . . . two . . ."

And now for the final knock . . .

"Three!"

Nothing.

"Cinderella, are you awake?" cries a voice from downstairs. "Where are you? Make us some tea!"

Oh, no! They're home!

And we're still here.

I hear the *clomp-clomp-clomp*ing of their walking around downstairs.

"I have to go," Cinderella whispers urgently, and turns to leave the room. "You guys have to get out of here!"

"We will," I say with more optimism than I feel. "There's still another mirror."

"Bye, Cinderella!" Jonah says.

"It was nice to meet you," I add.

I grab Jonah's hand. "This mirror is going to work. It has to. Ready? One . . . two . . ."

And now for another final knock . . .

"Three!"

Still nothing.

This is NOT good. Not good at all.

I hear more clomping. *Clomp-clomp-clomp* coming up the stairs.

The sisters are going to walk into their room any moment. We need to *do* something.

We need to hide.

I signal to Jonah for him to slide under the bed. It looks like I'm waving at him.

"Huh?" he says.

"Shh! And don't say huh. Say excuse me."

"Excuse me, what are you doing with your hand?"

Clomp-clomp-clomp.

"I'm trying to motion you to — Oh, forget it! Just slide under the bed!"

He nods and does it. Finally. I slide under Kayla's bed. The bed skirt reaches the floor, so unless they look for us, they won't catch us. Ouch! I just scraped the top of my arm.

What if they see us? What will we say? What will happen to us? Will they call the fairy tale police? Will we go to fairy tale jail?

The room is suddenly lit up.

"Cinderella, were you in our room?" someone asks in a high nasal voice. "Our door is open."

"Yes," Cinderella calls back. "I was, um, cleaning up." I hear footsteps coming closer — not the *clomp-clomp-clomp* kind, but the dainty kind. Cinderella's footsteps.

"Is that what you did all night?" the same person says.

"No. I was pretty busy," Cinderella says. I hear a smile in her voice.

At least she's not telling them the truth.

I hear the window opening and feel a flush of cool air. "So, tell me all about the ball," Cinderella says, and I detect a little bit of an edge to her voice. "Did either of you get to talk with Prince Jordan this time?"

Hmm. That wasn't very nice. She knows neither of them got to talk to the prince. She danced with him the whole time. Is Cinderella rubbing it in?

"Kayla got to talk to him," the same person — must be Beatrice — says.

"Really?" Cinderella says. "I didn't . . . I mean, that's nice. So what happened?"

"The beautiful stranger showed up again and interrupted them," Beatrice says.

"Really?" Cinderella says again.

"I heard she was a princess," Kayla says.

"She wasn't a princess," Beatrice says. "We'd have heard about her if she was a princess. I bet she was an heiress. Those clothes were expensive."

"The prince danced with her the rest of the night," Kayla says. "Again. I was really hoping she wouldn't show tonight."

"*Reeealllly?* The prince danced with the beautiful stranger? And that's why he stopped talking to you? How sad for you!"

I put two and two together and realize that the ordinary-looking girl we saw talking to the prince was Kayla. Also, is it just me, or is Cinderella being mean?

"Yes," Kayla says, "it was pretty sad." She sits down on her bed, and the mattress sags so that it's an inch from my face.

Uh-oh.

If she bounces, she's going to break my nose. DO NOT BOUNCE, KAYLA. DO NOT BOUNCE.

I hope she's not a bed jumper. I think back to all the times Jonah and I have jumped on our beds. What if there were kids from other dimensions hiding under our bed skirts and I had no idea?

My nose tingles.

Do not sneeze. Abby, whatever you do, DO NOT SNEEZE.

"Prince Jordan was *obsessed* with the beautiful stranger," Beatrice says. "He's in love with her, surely. How could he not be? She's gorgeous."

Ah-ah-ah —

Don't-don't-don't . . . I squeak a sneeze.

"Did you hear something?" Beatrice asks. "We better not have another mouse problem. Anyway, guess what happened at the end of the night?"

"I have no idea," Cinderella says. "Did Prince Jordan ask Kayla to dance?"

I can practically see Cinderella batting her eyelashes all fake-innocently.

"No," Kayla squeaks.

"Did he ask you to dance, Beatrice?"

"No," Beatrice huffs.

"I give up," Cinderella says.

"When the clock struck midnight, the beautiful stranger made a run for it. And no one could find her."

"No way," Cinderella drawls.

Way.

"The prince ran after her and found her glass slipper! It fell off while she was running, surely."

"Yes, it did," Cinderella says. Then she clears her throat. "It did?"

"Yes," Beatrice says, "And the prince is determined to find her. He'll be able to, surely."

Surely, surely, surely. She's such a know-it-all.

"I think I'll let you guys go to sleep," Cinderella says. "Or maybe you're not that tired. It doesn't sound like you did much dancing."

Yup, that was definitely mean.

She closes the door behind her. Uh-oh. She thinks we made it through the mirror. She thinks we're gone. And now we're stuck in the stepsisters' room! Argh!

I hear some shuffling on the bed above me. And then I hear . . . crying?

Why is one of the evil stepsisters crying? They're supposed to be evil, not sad.

The crying is coming from directly on top of me. It must be Kayla. The one who was talking with the prince.

"What on earth is wrong with you?" Beatrice asks.

"I just thought . . . I thought the prince might have liked me. I thought we had a connection."

"Oh, please. What did you expect? You can't compete with a girl like that. Get real. You're just not pretty enough."

My stomach hurts, and it's not from the pigs/dogs-in-a-blanket. I can't help but feel bad for Kayla. I know she's supposed to be evil and all, but she seems to really like Prince Jordan. And no one wants to like someone who doesn't like them back.

"Just go to sleep," Beatrice says, and the lights go back out.

Okay, at least they're going to sleep. Once they're out cold, Jonah and I can sneak out. They must be exhausted. It's well after midnight, their time at least. I have no idea what time it is at home, which is a little bit scary. I'm hoping time works the same way it did in *Snow White* — about one fairy tale day for every hour at home. Which means it's only about twelve thirty at home.

We just have to get home before Mom and Dad wake up, around seven.

Nothing I can do now. Nothing but wait.

And wait some more. When I finally hear not one but three sets of snoring, I decide it's safe to make a move.

I pull myself out from under the bed with my elbows and crawl over to Jonah. "Come on," I whisper. When he doesn't answer I give him a poke.

"What?" He jumps and hits his head on the mattress. "Ouch."

I shush him. When the sisters don't react, I motion to Jonah to follow me out the door.

I make the motion very, very clear.

He lifts his eyebrows, not getting it.

"Just follow me," I whisper, and roll my eyes. I carefully open the door. *Creeeak.*

We step into the hallway. Phewf!

The stepmom's door is closed. Guess she's asleep. How mean — she didn't even say good night to her daughters. I might be running out of underwear, but no matter how busy my parents are, they always come into our rooms to say good night.

"What do we do now?" Jonah whispers.

"I guess we go to sleep," I say. "Maybe Cinderella can help us find the right mirror tomorrow."

"But where will we sleep?"

I point to the winding stairs. "The attic. Cinderella's room."

When we reach the door, Jonah asks, "Should we knock?"

"Um, yeah." Now if he'd only knock on *my* door at home.

"But what if she gets scared?"

"She's probably already asleep," I say. "Hopefully, she has a couch up there we can curl up on. So I won't knock."

I turn the handle and quietly open the door. Cinderella is standing in the middle of the room, admiring the glass slipper.

"Hi," I say. "Glad you're still up."

Startled, she jumps. As she jumps, the glass slipper slips from her hands and drops directly onto her left foot.

"OWW!" she screams. "Ow, ow, ow!"

"Are you okay?" I ask, hurrying over to her.

"Do I look okay?" she snarls, holding onto her foot and hobbling over to a chair. "That really killed. You guys scared me. I thought you were gone!"

"The mirror didn't work," I say.

"Ow, ow, ow. That landed right on my foot."

"I'm so sorry," I tell her. "Do you want some ice?"

"It'll be okay. Just give me a sec. Ouch." She closes her eyes. "Only another day or so and then I'm outta here, right?"

"Right," I say. "Again, sorry."

"Can you bring me the slipper? Did it break?"

I look for the slipper on the ground and gulp when I see it. The heel has cracked off. In one hand, I'm holding a four-inch heel, in the other a flat glass boat. "It doesn't look so good," I admit.

Her eyes fly open. "Oh, boo," Cinderella says. "That isn't going to mess anything up, is it? The shoe being broken?"

"It shouldn't," I say, but I'm not so sure. "No — you have to try on the shoe the guy brings — at least, that's the way I remember it."

"The way you remember what the fairy told you?"

"Um, yeah. Right." I look around the room for a safe place to put the slightly broken shoe and rest it on top of the only shelf next to a tin bucket.

"Oh well." She closes her eyes again. "I'm really tired. And my foot really hurts. Like *really* hurts."

"It will feel better in the morning," Jonah says with a yawn. "That's what my mom always says."

"Then let's go to sleep," Cinderella says. "I have to be up in a few hours to make breakfast."

"Where's your bed?"

"I don't have one — I just sleep on the straw on the floor."

"That stinks," Jonah says. "You really need a mattress."

"I'll get one when I'm a princess," she says with a sigh.

"You'll get as many as you want when you're a princess," I tell her. "You can have a whole stack of them. Like *The Princess and the Pea*!"

"The who and the what?" she asks.

I shake my head. "Never mind."

"I hate peas," she adds.

"Forget I even mentioned them."

"Tomorrow," Cinderella says wistfully, "I'll be a princess."

"And we'll find our way home," Jonah adds.

"Everything will work out tomorrow," I say.

We each gather up some straw and mold it into beds. It's a little scratchy. Actually, a lot scratchy.

Well, at least I'm already in my pajamas.

* chapter nine *

This Isn't Looking Good

I wake up to the sound of screaming.

"My foot! Ouch, my foot! What happened to my foot?"

I bolt upright to see Cinderella clutching her left foot and howling.

"What's wrong?" I ask.

"My foot is wrong! Look at it!" She thrusts it in my face.

I have never seen a foot quite like this.

It is black.

It is blue.

Her toes are the size of marshmallows and the entire thing is bloated.

Is it a foot or a balloon?

"Is that from dropping the glass slipper on it?" Jonah asks.

"No, it's from playing the piano with my toes," she replies sarcastically. "Of course it's from dropping the glass slipper on it! It's completely swollen. And it hurts!"

I shake my head. "I knew we should have put ice on it."

She tries to stand up, but then grimaces and falls back down onto the straw. "How am I supposed to do my chores? I can barely stand."

"Cinderella! Cinderella! Where are you? Are you still sleeping?" yells a voice from downstairs.

"Oh, no," Cinderella wails. "That's Betty! My stepmother! I must have overslept! I have to make breakfast!"

Excuse me for a second. Betty? Her stepmother's name is Betty? That doesn't sound right. Betty sounds like a nana. Or someone who bakes cakes. It doesn't sound like an evil stepmother.

Cinderella tries to stand up again, but she winces as she puts weight on her foot. "I need to get dressed. And you two need to get out of here. I'm not allowed to have guests."

"Where are we supposed to go?" I ask. "We have to find the mirror that takes us home."

"You tried all the mirrors here," Cinderella says. "Go try other ones."

"But we don't know where else to go!" I say. "If the mirrors here don't work and the mirrors at the palace don't work, which mirrors will?"

Cinderella shakes her head. "I am not a mirror expert!" She hobbles over to the closet, opens the door, and stands behind it for privacy. When she closes it again, she's wearing a long-sleeved gray dress. "Now where did I put my shoes?"

"Your glass slipper?" Jonah asks.

"No, my work shoes. There they are." She spots a pair of loafer-like shoes at the door and limps toward them. She slides the right one on, no problem, and then tries to put on the left shoe. "Oh, crow, my foot is too swollen. I can't get the shoe on. I'm going to have to go barefoot."

Uh-oh.

I steal a look at the broken glass slipper that's lying by the wall. It's the right shoe.

Which means the prince has the left shoe.

If the loafer doesn't fit her left foot, then the glass slipper won't, either.

Crumbs.

If the glass slipper doesn't fit Cinderella, she isn't going to be able to prove she's the girl the prince danced with at the ball. They won't get married. She'll be stuck here forever.

I look at Jonah. He looks at me. He knows. He knows I know.

We did it again. We landed in a fairy tale and we messed things up.

Now what?

"Uh-oh," Jonah says. "Her foot is a basketball."

"Everyone shush!" I say. "I need to think. We need to fix this."

Cinderella waves her hand in the air. "Fix what? I feel like there's something you're not telling me here. Can you fill me in?"

I really don't want to.

"Your foot isn't going to fit the glass slipper," Jonah blurts out.

"It won't fit *today*," I say. "We'll take her to a doctor. Or it could still heal in time. We don't know when the prince is coming. Maybe he's not coming for another week. Her foot won't stay like this forever. It'll heal. It's probably not broken. It's probably just a sprain."

"Abby," Jonah calls out pointing to the wall. "It's okay! Look!" He's pointing at the slightly broken slipper on the shelf.

"We can show the prince's assistant that one. Cinderella will try it on her good foot and it will fit and our problem is solved."

Oh! Yay! "Jonah, you're right! Shoe problem solved!"

"Cinderella!" the voice from downstairs yells. It's getting closer. "You missed breakfast! We had to butter our own bread and brew our own tea! Where are you?"

"I'm coming!" Cinderella calls. "It's my stepmother!" she hisses to us. "She can't come in here! She'll see you!"

"Cinderella, I'm coming in," the voice says.

"Hide!" Cinderella whispers to us, her eyes wide with fear.

I look around the room. Hide where? There is nowhere to hide! There is just straw! No beds! No curtains! No nothing.

Oh, wait. There's the closet. We can hide in there. We'll be super quiet. She won't even notice us! We'll be invisible! Like mice! Instead of bothering to motion to Jonah, I jump up, grab his arm, and hustle toward the closet.

We can make it! We can make it!

The door to Cinderella's room swings opens just as Jonah and I are scrambling into the closet. I'm about to close the closet door behind us when — *Bam!* Jonah bumps his head into my back, I lose my balance, I fall against the wall, I extend out my arms try to stop myself from crashing to the floor, I knock over the tin bucket that's sitting on the shelf — and *clang! Smash!*

The tin bucket knocks over the only-slightly broken glass slipper. The only-slightly broken glass slipper crashes to the floor and smashes into a million pieces. It's now a VERY broken glass slipper.

Crumbs.

Shoe problem unsolved.

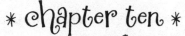

chapter ten

It Is Not a Pleasure to Meet You

Cinderella, what are you doing —" Betty stops in mid-sentence. "Excuse me! Young man! Young lady in the Floom flag! Who are you people?"

She's taller than I expected. Taller than Kayla. And scarier. She's wearing a long brown skirt and a tucked-in green blouse. She has thick straight gray hair that falls past her shoulders, straight bangs across her forehead, a narrow nose, thin lips, and beady brown eyes.

Betty definitely does not look like a Betty. A Betty would smile at me and offer me milk and cookies. Or maybe some brownies. A Betty would never glare at me like I was some sort of cockroach dashing across her floor.

Think fast, Abby, think fast. Why are we here? I know! When in doubt, be polite! "Hi," I say. "It's so nice to finally meet you."

"It is?" Jonah and Cinderella both ask.

"Jinx," Jonah calls.

Betty takes a step closer to me. "Who are you?"

"I'm Abby," I say, "and this is my brother, Jonah."

"We're from Smithville," Jonah adds.

Betty frowns. "And you are here, why?"

"Be-because . . ." Hmm. Long-lost cousins? I glance back at the bucket that unsolved my shoe problem and get an idea. "We're Cinderella's replacements!"

Betty clicks her tongue. "Do tell, why are we replacing Cinderella? Is she going somewhere?"

"As a matter of fact I am," Cinderella says haughtily. "I am going to —"

Oh, no! She can't mention the prince! "She's going to need help —" I interject while pinching Cinderella's arm.

"Ow!"

"— since she busted her foot. We're not really replacements," I add. "We're more like helpers."

Betty's beady brown eyes nearly bug out of her head at the sight of the overstuffed toes. "How did that happen?"

"Well," Cinderella begins. "Last night I dropped a glass sl —"

Nooooooo! "Sled," I interject, pinching her again. "She dropped a glass *sled* on her foot." Oops. That just came out.

"What is a glass sled?" Betty asks.

"You know," I say, stalling. "A sled. For sledding?"

"Down a hill!" Jonah adds. "I love sleds! We have one at home! It's wood, though. But I bet glass ones are slippier."

"Yes," I say. "Exactly. Much slippier." I really can't believe the words that are coming out of my mouth.

"But there's no snow outside. Where was she using a sled?" Betty asks. "And where did she get it?"

Right. Good points. "She found it in the neighbor's trash," I say. "Now we know why they were throwing it away. Dangerous things, these glass sleds. Especially when used down staircases."

Betty stares at me.

"Obviously she would have used it outside if there'd been snow," I add. "But there isn't." That kind of makes sense, doesn't it?

Do I sound as ridiculous as I think I do? Cinderella is bright red. Jonah is twisting his bottom lip. So yeah, I probably do.

Betty scans the attic. "Then where is said sled now?"

She's got me there. No. No, no, no. I will not let her win this! Where is the glass sled now? I know! "After it busted Cinderella's foot, I had to throw it out. Like the neighbors did. Wise people, those neighbors."

Jonah wags his finger like he's talking to a dog. "Bad sled. Bad, bad sled."

"But how did you two end up here?" Betty asks.

How did we end up here? Good question. I'm guessing that the magic mirror explanation isn't something I should share.

"She delivered the newspaper," Cinderella offers.

Way to go, Cindy! "Yes!" I cheer. "I was delivering the newspaper. Exactly. And I heard Cinderella scream when she landed at the bottom of the staircase."

"That makes no sense. Why is her foot swollen? You don't get swollen feet from falling down the stairs. You get a broken back or a concussion or —"

"Um, because when she picked up the sled to throw it out, she dropped it on her foot." There. Whew. "And then she screamed a second time, and I came running in. Your door was unlocked, by the way. Not a safe practice." Oh, I'm good! "She told me she had chores to do, so I offered to help her until she gets better."

Betty looks at me suspiciously. "Where are the rest of the newspapers?"

"We gave them out," I say quickly. "And then we came back."

Betty throws up her hands. "But why are you helping her? What's she giving you in return?"

"We're helping her because we're nice," Jonah says. "We don't mind. That's what nice people do. They help each other."

Betty's beady brown eyes narrow. She's not buying it. She doesn't understand what nice is! I need to speak her language. "Also," I add, "she's teaching us to speak English."

Betty raises an overly penciled-in and slightly uneven eyebrow. "It sounds to me like you already know how to speak English."

"She's teaching us to speak gooder," Jonah pipes up.

"Cinderella is a . . . a . . . a . . . *dortun jombi*," I say. "That's means 'good teacher' in Smithvillian. That's the language we speak in Smithville. Also —"

"Okay, I don't care," Betty says, looking bored. "If you want to help Cinderella while her foot is out of commission, knock yourself out. We're going to be busy, anyway. Since you delivered the paper, I assume you've all read the news?"

"Absolutely," I say, nodding. "Can you just remind us what it says?"

"Only that the prince has announced that he will marry whoever fits the glass slipper he found at the ball. His assistant will begin to visit all the households in the kingdom later today. So you three had better get started cleaning the house. Start in here. There's glass all over the floor."

Oh, no! Today already?

I look at Cinderella's foot.

Uh-oh.

"We have a *relamo*," Jonah says, after Betty leaves.

"A what?" I ask.

"*Relamo* is Smithvillian for problem," he says.

Hardy har har.

✳ chapter eleven ✳

We Need Magic, Pronto!

W hat are we going to do?" I ask.

"This really *is* a *relamo*," Cinderella says, frowning. "If the prince's assistant comes today, my foot is definitely not going to fit in the glass slipper."

"Right," I say.

"What should the Smithvillian word for 'trouble' be?" Jonah asks. "*Dessinsty?*"

"Jonah," I say. "Try to focus."

"Maybe he won't come today," Cinderella says wistfully. "Maybe he'll come tomorrow."

I check out the state of Cinderella's foot. "I don't think it's fitting tomorrow, either."

"So what do I do?" she asks. "I need it to fit!"

"You could always cut off one of your toes," Jonah says. "Like in the Grimm story."

Cinderella gasps. "That is, indeed, a grim story."

"Jonah, that's disgusting!" I say.

"I was just kidding," he says. "That would hurt. Although it would be really cool."

There has to be a solution. "Oh! I know!" I say. It's so easy! "You have a fairy godmother, right?"

Cinderella nods.

"So ask her to fix it! That's what she's there for. To fix things."

"I guess I could do that," Cinderella says.

"How do you get her to come?" Jonah asks. "Do you just call her?"

"Call her? Yes! Exactly. I call her name and she comes." Cinderella tilts her head toward the chimney, "Farrah! Farrah! Yoo-hoo, you there?"

"She's like Santa!" Jonah says.

A second later, a big puff of yellow is sparkling in the center of the room. Then the sparkle slowly trickles to the ground, and I see her — the legendary fairy godmother.

She is not what I expected. I thought she'd be plump.

But she's not. Instead, she's super skinny. And she has big wide eyes that are green and smiling. Her hair is wild and curly and perched on her head in a loose bun. Instead of wearing a twirly dress, she's wearing black leggings and a yellow sweater. She's like a human bumblebee. Or not human, exactly. Are fairies human? At least I think she's a fairy. I don't see any wings. She's holding a yellow-and-black swirly wand that looks like a candy cane. If candy canes were yellow and black.

"You're the fairy godmother?" Jonah blurts out.

"I am. And you must be Abby and Jonah."

"How did you know?" I ask.

She laughs. "Word gets around. So, Cinderella, what can I do for you?"

"You need to fix her foot," I say. "It's busted. It's never going to fit the glass slipper the way it is now. And if it doesn't fit the glass slipper, then she won't be able to marry the prince."

Farrah looks at Cinderella. "Is that what you want? To marry the prince?"

"Of course that's what I want!" Cinderella says. "Why do you think I wanted to go to the balls? For the pigs-in-a-blanket? I need the prince to rescue me and get me out of this place."

Farrah blinks. And then blinks again. "Excuse me?"

"I need him to rescue me," she repeats. "Marrying him will save me from this miserable life."

"And if you don't mind," I pipe in, "can you please direct us to the nearest magic mirror? We need to get home. Thank you for your time."

This is perfect. All of our problems will be solved with one burst of yellow sparkle! Farrah will fix Cinderella's foot and then send us home with a poof.

Farrah crosses her arms. "No."

"Exqueeze me?" Did I hear her right?

"No," she repeats.

Cinderella blinks. And then blinks again. "I don't understand. Why not?"

"First of all, I don't like being told what to do," Farrah says, glaring at all of us. "And second, Cinderella, I don't like this attitude of yours. Not one bit. You need to learn to rescue yourself! You need to learn to stand on your own two feet!"

"But my foot feels broken!" Cinderella whines. "I can't stand at all!"

"Well, you'd better learn. You can't rely on a prince to save you. You have to be self-reliant!"

"What's self-reliant?" Jonah asks.

"It means relying on yourself," I explain.

"I'm self-reliant," he says.

I snort. "Please. You don't even make your own bed."

"Does that mean you're not going to fix my foot today?" Cinderella asks meekly.

"I am not going to fix your foot today," the fairy godmother says. I can't believe how mean Farrah is being. None of the fairy tale versions mentioned this!

"We really need you to fix Cinderella's foot *today*," I say. "If the slipper doesn't fit, we won't be able to prove that Cinderella's the right girl! Isn't that why you sent her to the ball in the first place? So she could snag the prince?"

"Noooo," Farrah says. "I sent her so she could have a night out on the town!"

"You never thought that the prince might fall in love with her?" I ask.

"I'm fine with the prince falling in love with her — I just don't want her to be so needy about it." Farrah shakes her head at Cinderella. "You're not my only charge, you know. I'm the prince's fairy godmother, too. I've known him since he was a baby — no way do I want him getting stuck with a whiny damsel in distress. He needs a partner in his life. After all, a queen must be strong. If you can prove to me you won't be hanging on to his shirttails, I'll help you snag him. Got it? Show me you can stand on your own two feet and I'll fix your foot. I'm willing to help you — but only if you help yourself first."

"But it will be too late!" I say. "The prince's assistant is on his way now!"

"The assistant is at the other end of the kingdom. He won't make it here until Tuesday afternoon. I'll give you until Tuesday at noon to call for me and prove your self-reliance. It's Sunday morning. You have two and a half days. Make them count."

But — but — but . . . "Wait! Farrah? What about us? Can you help us find a magic mirror so we can go home?" I ask.

It's too late. She's gone in a puff of sparkle.

* chapter twelve *

Now What?

*t*here's no time for brainstorming ideas. We have to get right to work. Cinderella hobbles around the kitchen cleaning up the breakfast dishes while Jonah and I sweep the living room.

More precisely, I hold the dustpan while Jonah attempts to sweep.

He is the worst sweeper ever. He's just running around with the broom, swishing it in every direction. I think he might be making the dust worse than it was before.

"Focus, Jonah, focus!"

He sweeps a piece of dirt into my mouth.

"Jonah!" I say with a spit.

"Sorry," he says, but he's laughing so I don't really believe him.

His face turns serious and he twists his bottom lip. "Abby, how are we going to get home?"

"I, um, have a plan," I say. Although to be honest, I don't have a plan yet. I'm making it up right now. But I think it's important for Jonah to trust that I always have a plan. It's my job as the big sister.

"Yeah?" he says. "What is it?"

"Oh. Right. Well . . ."

"You don't have a plan, do you?"

"I do, I do! We help Cinderella prove to Farrah that she can be self-reliant before noon on Tuesday."

"What is it about twelve o'clock in fairy tales?" Jonah asks. "Whether it's noon or midnight, something always happens at twelve."

"That is true. I don't know why. So back to my plan. How about this — when Farrah comes back she'll be so amazed by the new and improved Cinderella that she'll happily tell us where the magic mirror is."

"But what if she doesn't know where it is?"

"She must know," I declare. "At the very least, she could zap us home herself. She does have a magic wand."

He nods. "Okay. Decent plan."

I hear footsteps in the hallway. It's Beatrice, the meaner sister. She looks a lot like her mother. Exact same thin nose and lips, exact same straight hair and bangs. Except hers is brown instead of gray. And she's the tallest of the three.

"Why are you two here?" she asks.

"We're here to help Cinderella."

"Good. Go help her with the wash. I'm low on underwear."

That makes two of us.

"Uh, okay."

"Kayla!" Beatrice yells up the stairs. "Do you need Cinderella to do your wash?"

"Yeah," Kayla calls back.

"The hampers are in our closet," Beatrice tells us. "We're going to visit friends now. Surely you'll see to it that the laundry is done by today so it'll be all ready for tomorrow. The prince's assistant is coming, you know."

"Fine." Must be a really slow washing machine.

I go upstairs. The stepsisters' door is closed so I knock. After what happened with Cinderella, I will never not knock again.

"Come in," I hear.

Kayla is lying facedown on her bed.

"Hi, Kayla," I say. "I'm just getting your laundry."

She turns her face toward me. "How do you know my name? Have we met?"

Well, I saw you fawning over the prince at the ball and then spied on you from under your bed. But no, technically, we haven't met. "You're Beatrice's sister, right?"

"Yes."

"We're helping Cinderella out while her foot heals," I say. "We're going to do your laundry and then make you dinner."

She nods. "Okay," she says, and then turns her head the other way.

"It's nice to meet you, too," I say sarcastically.

She doesn't bother to answer.

I bump Kayla's hamper down the stairs. "Cinderella?" I ask, popping my head into the kitchen.

But she's already done cleaning the kitchen and has managed to sweep and dustpan the entire marble entranceway by herself.

On one foot.

She's a cleaning machine.

"Wow," I say.

"Yes?" she asks.

"Where's the washer and dryer?" I ask.

"The what?"

"The washer and dr —" I stop in mid-sentence. "Do you guys not have a washer and dryer?"

"*I'm* the washer and dryer," she answers. "I wash the clothes by hand, then hang them up to dry."

Yikes. Even if my parents never bother using it, I have never felt more thankful for our washer and dryer in my entire life.

Cinderella and I are on all fours washing her stepsisters' clothes in the tub in the basement. At least they have running water in Floom, otherwise we'd be standing on a riverbank.

I'm soaping, Cinderella is rinsing, and Jonah is hanging. We have a whole production line going on. Next we're ironing wrinkled dresses. Cinderella is going to show me how to use the ironing board and everything.

"I don't understand what Farrah wants from me," Cinderella says. "How can I rescue myself?"

"Let's think about it," I say. "You said you were stuck here, right?"

"I *am* stuck here. I have nowhere else to go."

"But you're not chained to the house," I say. "You can leave if you want to."

"Where's your dad?" Jonah asks. "Is he dead?"

"He's not dead," Cinderella says. "He's just gone."

"Gone where?"

"Just gone. He left us. He left me. My mom's death was just too much for him."

"But he got married again," I say.

"I think he just wanted to find a place for me to live, since I was only twelve. And once he did — he took off. We used to get postcards, but we haven't heard from him in three years."

"That's terrible!" Jonah says. "I can't believe a dad would do that."

"He's a sailor," Cinderella says. "And he sailed away. I doubt I'll ever see him again. And he left me here. Stranded. I have no money and nowhere to go. That's why I need the prince to rescue me."

"Why don't you get a job?" I say, rinsing a pair of striped socks. "Then you'll have your own money and you can get your own house."

"But she's going to move into the palace when she gets married," Jonah says. "She doesn't need her own house."

"She won't get to marry the prince if Farrah doesn't fix her foot," I argue. "And Farrah won't help unless Cinderella helps herself. If Cinderella gets a job and moves out, it should prove to Farrah that she can be self-reliant. But if Farrah gets all weird and says it's not enough, at least this way Cinderella won't be stuck here anymore. It's a no-lose plan!"

Cinderella cocks her head to the side. "But what kind of job could I get? I'm not good at anything."

"That's not true," I say. "You're the world's fastest cleaner. You tidied that whole living room in forty-five seconds flat."

"You could be a cleaning lady!" Jonah says.

"We need to think bigger," I say, my eyes widening. "You could start a cleaning service! You could train a whole bunch of cleaners to clean superfast like you do and then send them out to people's houses! You taught us to clean; you can teach other people, too! You'll start a company. You'll make a fortune. You can call it . . . Mess Be Gone. No wait, Cinderella's Cleaners!" I pump my arm in the air, feeling proud of myself. I am a big fan of alliteration. Although I don't remember if alliteration has to be the same first letter or the same first sound. Whatever. It's still cute. From now on maybe I should go by Awesome Abby.

Cinderella shudders. "No way. I hate cleaning. I do it so fast so I can be done with it. I don't want to clean other people's houses for money. I don't want to clean this house, and if I had my own place, I wouldn't want to clean that, either. If I had my own money, I'd hire Cinderella's Cleaners."

"They probably wouldn't use your name if you weren't part of the company," Jonah points out.

Cinderella nods. "True."

I'm pretty sure she's missing an excellent business opportunity, but whatever. I think harder. "What about something with animals?" I say. "Aren't you really good with mice?"

"Farrah is good with mice, not me. Actually, I'm not all that great with any animal. Plus, I'm allergic to dogs. They give me a terrible cough and make me sneeze. Cats, too."

"Can you be a lawyer?" Jonah asks. "That's what our parents are."

"That takes a lot of schooling," I say, a little bit huffy. "Not everyone can be a lawyer, you know."

"I don't want to be a lawyer," Cinderella says. "Too much

arguing involved." She squeezes water out of one of Beatrice's shirts. "This is missing a button. I'll have to sew on a new one."

Hmm. "You can sew?"

She nods. "Of course. Can't you?"

"I've never tried," I say. "But I probably could. But this is about you. What about becoming a seamstress?"

"Think bigger," Jonah says, echoing my previous statement. "You could make clothes. You could be a fashion designer."

"That's perfect!" I say. Way to go, Jonah! "You'll make clothes and sell them. A perfect plan!"

"But what should I make?"

"You have to make something unique," I say. "Something that someone else isn't already making. What do you know how to make?"

Cinderella shrugs. "I've never made anything entirely from scratch, but I'm really good at stitching. I've hemmed skirts. Sheets. Shirts. Dresses."

"Can you make underwear?" I ask. Mine are giving me a wedgie.

"Um, I guess."

"Never mind. Let's focus on things people in Floom want."

"Floom people wear underwear," she says, sounding insulted.

87

"No, I mean special clothes," I say. I think about the people of Floom. What do they all like? Oh! "They loved your dress! Everyone loved the dress you wore to the ball. They couldn't stop gushing about it!"

She nods. "They did love my dress. I *loved* my dress. I wish I still had my dress."

Ding ding! "That's what you'll do! You'll make a Cinderella dress! You'll make a bunch of Cinderella dresses and then you'll sell them!"

"And make one for yourself," Jonah adds. "Maybe the prince's assistant will recognize you if you're wearing it when he comes by with the glass slipper."

Cinderella's eyes light up. "That, my little friend, is a perfect plan."

And once she's done with that, maybe she can make me a pair of jeans, a sweatshirt, and some new undies.

✳ chapter thirteen ✳

Project Cinderella

We take a break from the wash to search the house for material.

"The living room curtains!" I say. "They're platinum!"

"They're more of a silver," Cinderella says.

"Is there really a difference?" Honestly, I can't tell. "The curtains are perfect." It'll be just like in *The Sound of Music* when Maria makes the kids' clothes!

"I can't dismantle the curtains," Cinderella says. "Betty would notice."

"Is there anything else silver-ish that she has and won't miss?" I ask.

"I think she might have some extra tablecloths," Cinderella says. "Let's look in the closet."

We trudge over to the closet and find a stack.

"This one isn't bad," I say. "It's not exactly silver. It's more gray. But we can accessorize."

"But we still need to finish the wash," Cinderella says.

"We'll finish the wash," I say. "You make the clothes."

"I'll be in the attic," she says. "Wish me luck."

I peek into the room ten minutes later. "How's it going?"

"Great," she says from under the gray tablecloth.

"Did you sketch it out?"

"Um, no. Should I?"

"I think that's what designers do."

"I'm not really good at drawing," she says. "So I just started cutting."

"Okay," I say. She probably knows more about this dress stuff than I do. "What should we do next?"

"Can you make the beds?"

That I can definitely do. Unlike my brother, I make my own bed every morning.

Since Betty and the stepsisters have gone to "visit friends" (I know — they have friends? I'm shocked, too) I take my time making their beds and snooping through their stuff.

Kayla has *Jordan + Kayla* written in hearts all over her notebooks. I'd feel bad for her if she wasn't so mean.

I go back downstairs and find Jonah reading the newspaper at the kitchen table. And by the newspaper, I mean the comics. "Let's go," I say.

"Guess what I found," he says.

"Big Nate?"

"No, but there is a comic strip called Big Tate. Do you think they're related?"

"Maybe. Come on. We have to make the beds."

"Wait, I found something else you're going to like." He flips the pages back. "Look!"

Apartment in private home for rent
33 Slipper Street
Cozy, 600 square feet
Private bathroom, big kitchen, and big windows!
Ground floor! Great light! Wonderful location — near shops and palace.

No pets.

$100/month

"Isn't this perfect for Cinderella?" he says. "It's on Slipper Street. I think that's a sign. And no pets! She's allergic to pets."

"Rent is so cheap in Floom!" I say. "That's amazing!"

We clomp up the stairs to tell her the news.

"Sounds heavenly," she says.

I look around the room. All I see is a heap of tablecloth. "How's it going?" I ask, a little concerned. But she looks pretty intent, so I guess that's a good sign.

"Great. I'm a natural. I'll probably need another hour or so, though."

"Let us know if we can help! Good luck!"

An hour later: "Cinderella? How are you doing in there?"

"Wonderful! I need another hour! Do you think you could start dinner? Maybe make a chicken Caesar salad? We have leftover chicken from last night."

"Um, I don't know how to make Caesar salad," I say.

"Can't we just order a pizza?" Jonah asks.

"The cookbook is on the counter! It tells you how to make the dressing," Cinderella calls out.

"Oh. Okay."

How hard can it be?

We follow the recipe. We mince. We chop. We whisk. We finish the dressing. Then we make the salad.

"This was easier than I thought!" I say, munching on some loose lettuce.

And who knew? Cooking is fun! Cookbooks make it so much easier, though. Cinderella has the *Official Floom Cookbook*. There is a section on stew. There is a section on pizza. There is a section on something called *Kingslingions*, a Floom specialty, which calls for rice, shark fin, olives, and pineapple (which I never, ever want to try). There is also a section on desserts. Chocolate chip cookies! Lemon meringue pie! White chocolate cake! Yum.

When all the prep is done, we go back upstairs.

I knock and call from the hallway, "Cinderella? You still there? How's it going?"

"All done!" she says. "I'm just trying it on. Come in!"

"I can't wait to see it!" I squeal.

"Here I come!" She steps out from the closet and cheers, "Ta-da!"

Oh.

Oh, no.

It is not good.

It is not good at all.

The edges are jagged. The sleeves are uneven. There are random slashes in places that shouldn't have slashes. It looks about seven sizes too big.

She looks like the bride of Frankenstein.

She pirouettes. "Is it gorgeous? This was easier than I thought."

Jonah tugs at my arm. "That's what you said about making the Caesar salad."

Very true. Except the Caesar salad actually looks like Caesar salad. This dress does not look like the dress she wore to the ball. It doesn't look like a dress at all. It looks like a tablecloth that got attacked by a class of preschoolers with scissors.

Cinderella does another twirl. "I'll make you a pair of undies with the leftover material."

Thanks, but no thanks. "Cinderella, I don't know how to tell you this but —"

Her face falls. "What?"

I sigh. "You really need a mirror in here."

* chapter fourteen *

And the Next Plan Is . . . ?

"O h my," Cinderella says. We're in the stepsisters' room, examining the dress in one of the mirrors. She looks at herself from all angles. "Oh my, oh my. I am really not a good designer."

"No," I say. "You're really not."

"You can keep practicing," Jonah says. "You don't get good at something overnight."

"That's true," I say. "But it's already Sunday evening. It's almost dinnertime. We only have a day and a half left to raise a hundred dollars!"

Cinderella sighs.

"What?" I ask.

"It just seems like an awful lot of work for something that's not going to be needed in the end. I mean, if this convinces Farrah to help me, I'm going to marry the prince and live in the palace. I won't need the apartment after all."

"You could keep the apartment for your office," Jonah says.

She makes a sad face. "My office for what?"

"Your job," I remind her. "I want to get married one day, but I still want to be a judge. Even if you do marry the prince, you might discover you like being self-reliant. Even a princess should feel self-reliant. In the meantime, you still need a job. Are you sure you don't want to be a cleaning person? Or maybe just a clothes washer?"

"I hate washing clothes," Cinderella says. "My hands are all chapped. And it's boring. I want to *make* something."

"You're making something cleaner," I say.

Cinderella shrugs. "Is the chicken Caesar salad done?"

"Yup. All set.

"Oh, good. Did you make anything for dessert?"

"No, were we supposed to?"

"I can do it. But we'd better hurry. They'll be home soon, and they eat at seven."

My stomach grumbles. "When do *we* eat?"

"After they eat."

"Oh, man," Jonah wails. "I'm hungry."

We help Cinderella back down the stairs and into the kitchen. We hear the front door open, and then Betty butts her head in. "I hope dinner is almost ready," she says.

"Gezuty!" Jonah says.

"Hmm?"

"That's Smithvillian for 'almost,'" he explains.

She rolls her eyes and steps out.

"So what should we make?" I ask, flipping through the cookbook. "Cake? Lemon meringue pie? Cookies?"

"What about brownies?" Jonah asks.

"Yum, I love brownies," I say. "Let's make them."

Cinderella's face scrunches up. "What are brownies?"

Both my brother's and my jaws fall open. "What are brownies?" I yell. "Are you joking?"

She shakes her head. "I've never heard of them."

"You've never tried a chocolate brownie?" Jonah repeats, dumbfounded.

"I've never tried any kind of brownie," she says with a shrug.

"You really need to get out more," I say. "I'm sure they're in the book." I flip through the pages. Cinnamon cupcakes, pineapple tarts, chocolate chip cookies, apple muffins . . . but no brownies. NO BROWNIES?

"I can't find a single brownie recipe. This should be illegal."

"What is a brownie, exactly?" she asks.

"It's a small square of deliciousness," I say.

"So let's make some," Cinderella says. "Do you know how?"

"It's easy," Jonah says. "You take the brownie mix off the shelf and give it to your mom and dad and they mix it with some stuff." His face falls. Either he just realized that Cinderella doesn't have any brownie mix or he remembered that our parents don't have much time for brownie making right now.

"Oh," he says. "I guess that won't work. You probably have to make it from scratch."

"So what's the recipe?" Cinderella asks.

I look at Jonah. He looks at me. "I don't know," I say. "Our parents never made them from scratch."

"Okay, why don't you tell me what it tastes like?" Cinderella asks. "Maybe I can figure it out."

"They're chocolaty. They're like a cross between a cookie and a cake," I say.

Cinderella ties an apron around her waist and pulls out a mixing bowl. "I do a lot of baking, so we'll have some trial and error. Do you mind being my tasters?"

"That is something I wouldn't mind at all," Jonah says. "Bring on the brownies!"

Hmm. I'm getting an idea here. "You do a lot of baking?"

"Yup," she says, turning on the oven. "Lots."

"Do you like baking? Is it something you could do even more of?"

"Sure," she says. "I find it relaxing."

Here's the big one: "Are you any good at it?"

"I'm not bad," she says with a shrug.

"Are you a better baker than you are a sewer?" I ask.

She laughs. "Much better. Are you guys thinking what I'm thinking?"

My mind is racing. "I'm thinking that this could be your job! You can bake brownies and sell them! All of Floom would come and buy them because you're the only person who makes them."

"Where would I sell them?" Cinderella asks.

"Your apartment!" I say. "It'll be an apartment *and* bakery. It's on the ground floor — it's perfect."

"You want me to start my own shop?"

"Yes! Wouldn't that be cool? You could call it Cinderella's Brownies! Wait. No. That doesn't have alliteration. Hmm. It's really too bad you're not making cookies. Cinderella's Cookies has alliteration." Maybe not alliteration. But close enough.

"Floom already has cookies," Cinderella says.

I drum my fingers against the counter. "Right. And you have cakes and cupcakes, too, huh?"

She nods. "We do."

"Oh, well. Brownies it is. I'll keep thinking about the name."

"But I need to sell these brownies before I have the money to get the apartment," Cinderella says. "I guess we could sell them at the market. We could set up a booth."

"Perfect!" I say. "We'll go tomorrow!"

"Hurray!" Jonah cheers.

"Our problems aren't solved yet," Cinderella says, her forehead wrinkling. "I still don't know how to make the brownies."

Oh. Right. "You will. I have complete faith in your baking skills."

I hope I don't have to eat those words.

* chapter fifteen *

If At First You Don't Succeed, Keep Eating

While Cinderella bakes in the kitchen, Jonah puts the chicken Caesar salad on plates and I serve it in the dining room.

"You didn't give me enough chicken," Beatrice complains.

Excuuuuuuuse me.

"Do you want me to get you more?" I ask.

"Surely I do. Why else would I have complained?"

Um, because you complain about everything? So far she's told me that there's:

1. A speck of dirt on her fork.

2. A draft in the room.

3. No pepper on the table.

"Anything else?" I ask. I look at Kayla, but she's too busy staring at her plate. What's up with her?

"You need to refill our water, too," Betty snaps. "I'm thirsty."

"No problem," I say with fake cheer. As long as they're not coming in the kitchen, I'm happy.

I keep a fake smile on my face until I'm back in the kitchen and then groan. "Betty and Beatrice are so annoying. More water! More chicken! Clean forks! Blah, blah, blah!"

"Don't forget about Kayla," Cinderella says, pulling her first batch of brownies from the oven. "Hasn't she complained about the food needing more salt yet? She always complains about the food needing more salt."

"She hasn't actually." Kayla's barely said two words. She's barely eating, either. She's just moping into her food.

"Maybe she's getting sick or something," Cinderella says. She cuts out two chunks of brownie and hands one to Jonah and one to me. "Here, try this."

"Blah," Jonah says, spitting it out in the garbage.

"Jonah, that's so rude," I say.

"But it tasted gross!"

"Can you try to be constructive, please?" I ask.

He looks thoughtful. "It needs to be less bad."

I take a small bite. I second the blah, but keep it to myself.

"Very constructive, Jonah, thank you. I actually think it needs more sugar. And maybe more chocolate chunks."

"Will do," Cinderella says, dancing around the kitchen. I think she's having fun. Now all we need is for her to make a decent brownie and we'll be all set.

The next batch is disgusting, too. And way too gooey. I didn't know it was possible to have brownies that were too gooey, but it is.

"Should I feed it to the evil ones for dessert?" I ask.

"Yes," Jonah says. "Maybe it will make them barf."

I shudder. "But then we'd have to clean up the barf."

"I actually don't know what to give them for dessert," Cinderella says. "We have nothing ready."

"Do you have any fruit?" I ask.

"Fruit isn't dessert," Jonah says, looking horrified.

"It is, too," I say. "I saw some clementines. They can have those."

"Make sure to peel them," Cinderella says.

"Seriously?" I groan. "Jonah, help me."

"I'm kinda busy," he says. By busy he means, he's dipping his finger in the brownie bowl and licking it. "After you make chocolate brownies, can you make caramel brownies? And chocolate chip brownies? And blondies?"

"And some with nuts," I add.

"Yuck," Jonah says. "No one really likes nuts in their brownies. They just eat them because they have to."

"Why would you have to eat brownies with nuts?" I ask.

"Parents think they're healthier. Like carrot cake. People think it's healthy just because it has carrots in the name. Blah. Please do not put nuts in your brownies."

"Got it," Cinderella says. "No nuts."

"And no carrots," Jonah adds.

The clementines do not go over well.

"Fruit is not dessert!" Beatrice cries.

"I expect you to make something more dessert-y tomorrow," Betty says. "There are three of you in there. You have no excuse."

Grumble, grumble, grumble.

Kayla just stares at her clementines.

Back in the kitchen I discover that batch three of the brownies is burnt.

I'm beginning to get nervous.

"What about ketchup brownies?" Jonah suggests.

"That's disgusting," I say. "And stop eating the brownie mix!"

"I think these need vanilla," Cinderella says, sampling batch four. I've just cleared the plates off the dining room table.

I have no idea what vanilla does to brownies, so I am happy to take her word for it.

"Cinderella?" Kayla says, poking her head into the kitchen. "I'd like another glass of water."

Seriously? Can she not pour the water herself?

"Of course," Cinderella says.

Kayla eyes the many plates of brownies. "What are you doing in here?"

"Preparing dessert for tomorrow," Cinderella answers, which is not a lie.

"Oh," she says. She looks like she's about to say something more, but she doesn't. When Cinderella hands her a glass of water, though, she whispers a tiny "Thank you." Then she hurries out of the kitchen.

Cinderella looks stunned. "What was *that*?" she says. "Kayla never says thank you. None of them do."

"That's so rude," I say.

"That's the least of it," Cinderella says. "Last week Kayla dripped tomato sauce on the chair and then blamed me. Betty made me scrub it with my toothbrush. She and Kayla just laughed. Then Beatrice spilled more on purpose. The two of them are the worst. Sure, Beatrice's usually the instigator but Kayla's no angel."

I put my arm around her thin shoulders. "You'll be out of here soon. I know it."

"You will," Jonah says, helping himself to another spoonful of batter. "This stuff isn't bad. It's not as awesome as dogs-in-a-blanket but —" His eyes light up. "Can you make dogs-in-a-blanket brownies? That would be awesome."

"Please don't," I say.

"We could dip them in ketchup!"

Sometimes I'm not sure how we're even related.

Cinderella finishes batch five at around eleven.

I chew carefully. It is chocolaty. It is the perfect amount of gooey. It is melt-in-my-mouth delicious. Hurray!

"Cinderella," I say slowly. "This is the best chocolate brownie I have ever had in my entire life."

The next morning, we wait for Betty and her daughters to leave to visit more friends before we start baking. (I know — more friends?)

We use up all the chocolate and all the flour and all the eggs and make ten trays of brownies — one dozen brownies per tray. We wait for them to cool down, pack them up, and get ready to go to the market.

If we sell them for a dollar each, we'll even have extra money. Cinderella is going to need extra cash for supplies and stuff.

Except . . .

"Um, guys?" I ask. We're all ready and standing in front of Cinderella's house. We have the brownies, some signs, and even the ironing board. That was my great idea. We need some sort of table for the booth, right? "Where is the market? And how are we supposed to get there?"

"Cinderella," Jonah says. "Don't you have a car or something you can drive?"

She shakes her head. "My coach turned into a squashed pumpkin, remember?"

"How do you normally get there?" I ask.

"I normally walk. It's not that far. Maybe twenty minutes. No problem."

"Um, yes, problem. We're carrying ten trays of brownies." I look down at her still swollen foot. "Even if Jonah and I carry your share, I don't think we're walking anywhere."

"Maybe she can stay behind and bake more brownies?" Jonah asks. "And we can do the selling?"

"I don't know if that's gonna cut it with Farrah," I say. "How is she walking on her own two feet if we're leaving her behind?"

We stand there, not sure what to do.

One coach goes by us. And then another one.

"Can we call a taxi?" Jonah asks.

"A what?" Cinderella asks.

Hmm. If this brownie thing doesn't work out, she can start a taxi service.

"We can always take the parriage," Cinderella says.

"I hate porridge," Jonah says. "Stick to brownies, please."

"The what?" I ask.

"The parriage! Don't you have parriages in Smithville?"

"I don't know what that is," I say.

She looks at me with disbelief. "This Smithville place sure sounds backward."

Humph. At least we have brownies.

"Oh, look," she says, pointing down the street. "Here comes a parriage now!"

Up ahead is a green carriage being pulled by two horses. On the front of the carriage it says 5: CROSSTOWN.

"Oh!" Jonah exclaims. "It's a bus!"

"It's a parriage," Cinderella says. "You know. Public carriage."

"Cool," I say. "But how much does it cost? We don't have any money."

"Fifty cents a person," she says. "Each way."

"Maybe we can pay in brownies." I wave at the driver as the parriage approaches, but he doesn't stop.

"Don't be silly," Cinderella says. "You have to be picked up at the parriage stop."

"Where is it?" I ask, annoyed. We're never going to make it!

"At the end of the street," Cinderella says.

I see a sign in the shape of a diamond at the corner. "Jonah, you run, and I'll help Cinderella. Go, go, go!"

Jonah runs up ahead, carrying his share of the brownies. I don't know if he's going to make it.

Cinderella and I follow behind as fast as we can.

"Ouch," she says with every step. "Ouch, ouch, ouch."

"We're almost there!" I encourage. Poor Cinderella.

He runs . . . he runs . . . and he makes it!

Jonah steps onto the carriage. He steps back out a second later. "He'll take us," he shouts. "For a half dozen brownies!"

"Six brownies? That's highway robbery! That's six dollars' worth!"

"It's worse than that. I had to give him a whole brownie to taste first. He liked it — a lot — but that's his final offer. He says take it or leave it."

"It's not like we have a choice," Cinderella says.

Grumble. Sounds like brownie blackmail to me. "All right. Six more brownies it is," I say. I wish we had saved some of our gross ones from last night.

We reach the bus, hand over the brownies, and squish into a seat.

"These are really good," the driver says. Crumbs are caught in his beard. "What are they called again? Crownies?"

"Brownies," Jonah says.

Hmm, I kind of like *crownies*. And since no one here knows what brownies are we can call them *crownies* if we want. Why not? We invented them! And then we could call the store Cinderella's Crownies!

"Cinderella's Crownies," I announce. "We'll be at the market. Tell your friends."

Cinderella puts her foot up on the seat. Her toes are still the size of marshmallows.

Hmmm. Marshmallow crownies?

I look back at her toes. Yuck. Never mind.

* chapter sixteen *

Step Right Up

the market has all kinds of cool stuff. Food, clothes, furniture, old people in puffy outfits. We set up on the ironing board. Jonah hangs a sign that says, CINDERELLA'S BROWNIES! $1 EACH!

I take out the marker and turn the *B* into a *C*. Much better.

The brownie-crownies look amazing. They smell amazing.

Only problem? We've sold:

Zero.

"Why is no one buying any?" Jonah whines, finishing off a brownie-crownie.

"Maybe they're too expensive," Cinderella says.

"Yes, but this way we don't have to sell as many," I say.

"Yes, but right now we're not selling any," she says. "If they cost less, more people will buy them."

When did she get so business-savvy? "Fine. We'll try selling them for fifty cents apiece."

I change the sign to two for a dollar. It doesn't help.

Do you know what's also not helping? Jonah eating all the brownie-crownies.

"What time does the market close?" I ask.

"We have a few more hours," Cinderella says. "We have to get home and make dinner."

"At least we have dessert," Jonah says.

One older woman comes up and sniffs at the table. "What are you selling?" she barks.

"Brownies!" Jonah says.

"Crownies!" I correct him. "Would you like to buy two? Only one dollar."

"What's a crownie?"

"It's a yummy dessert!"

"No, thanks," she says, and walks away.

"You don't know what you're missing!" Jonah calls out after her and helps himself to another brownie-crownie.

Wait a sec. "That's the problem!"

"What is?" Jonah asks.

"They don't know what a crownie is!" I say.

"No one knows what a crownie is," Jonah says. "It's not a real word."

I ignore him. "They don't know how good crownies are. We need to give them samples. That's what you did to convince the parriage driver, right? It'll work here, too!"

"You want us to give away crownies for free?" Cinderella asks eyes wide.

I nod. "Except not whole ones. We'll cut them even smaller. Once people taste them, they'll buy them! It'll be like Whole Foods or Costco! I love when they give you samples. Jonah, you'll go into the crowd and pass them out. Make sure to tell them that we're selling them right here, okay?"

He salutes me. "Aye, aye, captain."

I break some crownies into pieces, put them on a plate, and hand them to my brother. "And, Jonah —"

"Yeah?"

"No munching!"

*   *   *

We've given away a total of twenty crownies in samples. And we've sold ten crownies at fifty cents each. Meaning, we've made five dollars. Except we're out ten dollars in merchandise.

"It's better than nothing," Cinderella says.

"True," I say. "Rome wasn't built in a day."

"What's Rome?" she asks.

"You really need to get out more," I say.

"I'm out of samples," Jonah says, coming back to our booth.

"We definitely have more of those," I say. "Wanna switch?"

"Sure," he says.

I cut up the crownies into even smaller pieces and start walking down the rows. There's a butcher selling meat. A couple selling silver necklaces that have a dangling green eye on them. A little bit creepy. Oh! A woman with red hair is selling seriously cute dresses for ten dollars! I wish I had money so I could get one. Right now I'm wearing one of Cinderella's drab gray dresses. It's kind of itchy. And about two sizes too big.

"Crownies!" I chant. "Come have a free crownie! A brand-new dessert like you've never had before! It's a mix between a cookie and a cake! The chocolate will melt in your mouth! Goes great with a glass of milk!"

A few people take samples and I remind them to come by our booth.

"I'll try one," says a little freckled boy.

I hand him one and watch as his eyes widen with joy. "Delicious!" he says.

"Excuse me, would you like a tasty treat?" I offer a pregnant woman. "We're selling them for fifty cents at our booth!"

"Absolutely," she says. "Hey, these are amazing!"

I give her an extra one since she's tasting for two.

"Excuse me, would you like to taste Cinderella's Crownies?" I say to the back of a young woman's head. "They're delicious! They're homemade! Come meet the baker!"

She turns around.

Her hair isn't blond or brunette. It's in the middle. And frizzy. Her eyes aren't blue or green or sparkly or really big. They're average. And her lips are kind of thin.

My jaw drops.

Her jaw drops.

It's Kayla.

✳ chapter seventeen ✳

Nowhere to Hide

AGHHHH!

The first thing I think is: *RUN, ABBY, RUN!*

So I run.

I run past the redheaded dressmaker and the butcher.

Maybe she'll think she imagined me? I run and duck and stop and hide behind a group of teenagers and then run some more. I don't want to return to Cinderella's Crownies in case Kayla is following me. I can't lead her to the evidence!

I crouch to the ground behind a cookie booth to catch my breath. She's probably not following me. She probably didn't even see me. And I ran really far. I definitely lost her. I'm a really good spy.

I stand up carefully. Mmm. Those cookies smell good. I wonder if I could trade a brownie sample for a chocolate chip cookie?

I look across the counter. Kayla is staring right at me.

"Hi, Abby," she says.

It's over. Kayla is going to tell her mother. They'll drag us home and lock Cinderella and Jonah and me in the attic, and Cinderella's Crownies will be over before it ever really began.

"What are you doing here?" Kayla demands. "What are Cinderella's Crownies?"

"They're . . . they're . . ." I try to come up with some sort of lie, but instead I shove the plate under her nose. "Try one."

She shrugs. Takes a bite. Chews. "Wow," she says. "These are great! Crownies, they're called?"

"Excuse me," says the cookie lady. "Would you mind going to the other side of the counter? We're selling cookies here, not cookie imitations. Please remove yourself from the premises."

These are crownies, not cookie imitations, thank you very much. I walk around the counter to Kayla.

"Yup," I say to Kayla. "Crownies."

"And Cinderella made them?"

I nod.

"I'm impressed! And she's selling them at the market?"

I hesitate but nod again.

"What for? Oh, I know. I bet she's trying to make money so she can move out."

My mouth drops open. "How did you know?"

She shakes her head. "It's not easy living with my mom. And my sister's no picnic, either. I should know."

I can't help but be surprised. "What do you mean? Don't you like living with them?"

"I don't have a choice. I can't leave my mother and sister. But Cinderella can. She should. They treat her like a slave!"

"Um, she does your laundry, too. And makes your meals. And your bed. You kind of treat her like a slave, too."

Her cheeks turn red. "I guess you're right. I shouldn't. I don't mean to." She sighs. "But you're right. I do. Correction. I *did*."

"I don't understand. How have you only realized this now? It's been going on for years!"

She sighs again. "This is going to sound strange, but something unfair happened to me recently and it made me think about all the other unfair stuff that happens all the time."

I wonder what she's talking about. I guess she means what happened with the prince. "Unfair stuff happens all the time," I say, "but what's happening to Cinderella is super unfair."

"I know." She bites her lower lip. "How can I help?"

"You really want to help?" I want to believe her. I really do. But what if she's setting us up?

"I really, really do," she says, eyes wide.

"What about your mom and sister? Are they here?"

"No, it's just me. They dropped me off. Told me I was moping too much. Told me to buy something to make me feel better. I picked up a new pair of shoes." She motions to her satchel. "I'm taking the parriage back home later."

I give her a long, hard stare. She seems earnest. I want to believe her, really I do. But I don't want to be gullible. "Okay," I say, finally. "You can help."

I'll give her a chance, but I'm still going to keep an extra-special eye on her.

Maybe I need one of those creepy green eye necklaces after all.

"Step right up, step right up!" Kayla hollers. "Cinderella's crownies for sale!"

I can't believe it — Kayla is selling Cinderella's crownies. And she's selling a lot of them. She's a natural. She even bought a few for herself — for a dollar each! It was her idea to jack up the price back to a dollar.

Jonah and Cinderella almost had heart attacks when I brought Kayla over, but I vouched for her and so far so good.

It seems she really has changed. I do feel bad that she's still pining for the prince. But Cinderella and the prince are meant-to-be. You can't get in the way of meant-to-be.

I'm sad she's sad, but I'm also happy she's becoming a nicer person. Sometimes tough experiences change you for the better, I guess.

"Cinderella, your crownies are really amazing," she says.

Cinderella flushes with pleasure. "Thank you. It means a lot to hear you say that."

"I'm sorry I don't say nice things more often. I've been the worst stepsister ever."

"Well . . ." Cinderella hesitates.

"Yes," I fill in for her. "You have been."

"I've had it so easy and you've had it so tough," Kayla says. "I'm sorry."

I wonder if she'd still feel sorry if we told her the *whole* plan. All she knows is that we're trying to raise a hundred dollars so Cinderella can move out. She has no idea that Cinderella wants to move out to prove to Farrah that she can rescue herself. No clue whatsoever that Cinderella wants to marry the prince, who just happens to be the guy Kayla is pining for.

"You haven't had it *that* easy," Cinderella says. "Your dad died when you were really little, and you have to share a room with Beatrice, who's incredibly bossy. And your mom . . . well, your mom is really . . ."

"Mean?" I say.

Kayla snorts. "That's the understatement of the year. She yells at puppies. What kind of a person yells at puppies? But at least I have my own money. My dad set up a big trust fund for me and my sister. I don't have to rely on anyone for anything."

"Still," Cinderella says, "it must be tough being in your shoes."

I look down at Kayla's shoes. They're black and shiny. They're definitely nice. They're also really big. Her feet are about twice the size of Cinderella's. Even the swollen one.

No, the glass slipper is definitely not fitting on *her* foot.

"I need another crownie," she says. "Here's a dollar."

I hand her an extra-chocolaty one. "Don't worry," I say. "This one's our treat."

* chapter eighteen *

Keep On Bakin'

even though we sold most of our crownies, we only made thirty dollars. Then we had to use ten dollars of that money to buy more crownie ingredients, which only left us with twenty dollars' profit.

Which means we have to go back to the market tomorrow morning and make eighty dollars. Which seems kind of impossible.

And we only have until noon at the latest.

Then I subtract the time it takes to get to and from the market, and I get really worried. "Do you think Farrah would meet us at the market at noon?" I ask.

Cinderella shakes her head. "She really seems to like chimneys and fireplaces."

Long story short? That night, instead of sleeping, we bake.

Chocolate chip crownies, blondies — or *clondies* as we call them — and walnut crownies, even though Jonah keeps shaking his head in disapproval.

It's a good thing I'm busy mixing ingredients all night, because there's no way I can sleep. I'm way too nervous. What if our plan doesn't work? Will Farrah think we failed our mission? Will she not help Cinderella? Will she not help Jonah and me get home?

We really have to get home. Technically it's only been a few days in fairy tale land, so probably only a few hours have passed at home.

The key word here is *probably*.

What if I'm wrong? What if time is going faster at home? What if *days* have passed? Or what if Farrah doesn't help us find the magic mirror that will lead us back to Smithville? Then what?

Then we're stuck in Floom . . . forever.

It's seven o'clock Tuesday morning. I'm navigating through the many booths at the market. Jonah and Cinderella have been here since six. I stayed behind to wait for the last two batches of crownies to cool and to leave the stepfamily their breakfast.

But who knows what'll happen when Betty wakes up and realizes we're not there. We asked Kayla to tell her that we had some errands to run. I hope Kayla doesn't change her mind and tell on us.

As we approach our booth, I feel an explosion of butterflies in my stomach. What if it's slower than yesterday? What if no one buys anything? What if we can't pull it off?

Wow, it's really busy here today. Look at that booth near the entrance! They have a line. It snakes around the block.

I wonder what they're selling?

As I step closer to the booth, I realize something amazing.

The people are standing in line for Cinderella's Crownies.

By nine o'clock, we've sold forty crownies.

By ten, sixty-five.

By eleven-thirty, we're sold out.

We've made a hundred and twenty dollars.

"You did it!" Jonah cheers, giving Cinderella a high five.

We actually had six crownies left, but we let ourselves have a snack. Of course, the six crownies left had walnuts. But that didn't stop Cinderella *and* Jonah from eating their share. I'm saving one of mine for later.

"*We* did it," Cinderella says. "You guys are the best. I couldn't have done it without you."

That's true, though technically she shouldn't have had to do it at all. It's because of us she hurt her foot. No need to remind her of that, though. "You're going to be a princess!" I tell her instead.

Cinderella puts the money in an envelope, which I carry in one of the extra satchels.

We give each other a group victory hug and then run, run, run to catch the parriage.

The grandfather clock in the living room says 11:45 when we open Cinderella's front door. We only have fifteen minutes left to call Farrah!

"Where have you been?" Betty snaps when we step inside. "The prince's assistant is on his way and I had to prepare the tea myself!"

Oh, no. I don't want to anger Betty. What if she somehow messes up the plan?

"We were at the market," Cinderella says.

"Doing what?" Betty barks.

"Getting dinner." It's the truth. Cinderella bought a pot roast from the butcher for later. Betty has an account there, so she charged it.

Though if everything goes her way by the time dinner rolls around, she won't be the one cooking it. She'll be engaged to the prince.

Betty looks at her with suspicion.

"We just need to freshen up," Cinderella says, "and then we'll make lunch."

"What *I* need is for you to finish preparing the tea and cakes for the prince's people. I've just heard that they're only a few houses away. They should be here within the hour. So you need to hurry. Beatrice and Kayla are making themselves presentable as we speak."

"We'll be right down," Cinderella says cheerfully.

It's 11:50.

Jonah and I run up the stairs while Cinderella hobbles up behind us. We pass Beatrice and Kayla's room on the way. Their door is open, and I peek inside.

"Cinderella!" Beatrice yells. "I need your help!"

"Can't now," Cinderella says, giving Kayla a thumbs-up.

Then up to the attic we go. We close the door behind us.

Cinderella knocks on the chimney. "Farrah? Are you there?"

My heart races. I hope this works. It HAS to work.

There's a burst of yellow sparkle. Here we go.

✳ chapter nineteen ✳

Now or Never

So," Farrah says, twirling her wand between her fingers like it's a cheerleading baton. "How'd you do?"

"She did great!" I say, but then wonder if I should let Cinderella do the talking. A person who stands on her own two feet should definitely use her own tongue, right? "I'll let her tell you about it."

Farrah nods. "Good idea."

Cinderella takes a step forward. "We decided I would get a job so I could afford an apartment of my own. And Jonah — um, I mean *we* — found a great place that's a hundred dollars a month. You said that if I could prove to you that I can rescue myself, you would fix my foot. And if you fix my foot, then I'll fit the glass slipper like Abby said I was supposed to. So I started a crownie company called Cinderella's Crownies to raise a hundred dollars for the apartment."

"What's a crownie?" Farrah asks.

Jonah rolls his eyes. "It's really called a brownie. My sister's just weird."

"Crownies are little square cakes," Cinderella explains. "I baked a bunch and then we sold them at the market. I really enjoyed making them and selling them, and we made a hundred and twenty dollars, which is enough to —"

"Rent an apartment!" I shriek. I'm sorry. I'm just not good at containing myself. "Which proves she can stand on her own two feet! She's self-reliant! She is, she is!"

"Exactly," Cinderella says.

Farrah nods. "I'm impressed. You can afford to rent your own apartment? That does prove to me that you're not just a damsel in distress. Maybe you're a worthy partner for the prince after all."

"Yay!" I cheer. "And, Farrah, not that I'm not focusing on Cinderella and her issues right now, but we really need to talk about finding a magic mirror."

She smiles. "Let's take care of Cinderella first, okay?"

She lifts her wand. She makes three circles in the air and then sends a zap toward the table. The glass slipper that had been smashed reappears in a puff of sparkle. Oh, yay! She fixed it!

"And now for your foot," she says.

Yes, yes, yes! Everything is going to be back on track now. Hurray!

The door bursts open. "Not so fast. Stop whatever you're doing!"

Betty! What is she doing here? Beatrice is behind her. Beatrice and . . .

Kayla.

"See, Kayla?" Beatrice says, pointing to the glass slipper on the table. "I told you she was the mystery girl from the ball. She stole your prince!"

"How did you know?" Cinderella asks.

"It wasn't that hard to figure out," Beatrice says. "Also I'm a very good eavesdropper. You guys aren't exactly quiet."

Kayla's eyes tear up. "I don't understand. I thought you were trying to raise a hundred dollars so you could move out."

"Technically, she was raising a hundred dollars to prove to me that she's worthy of the prince," Farrah says.

"You lied to me," Kayla says, her mouth turning down. "You stole my prince!"

"I'm sorry, Kayla," Cinderella says. "But he was never *your* prince. If he was your prince, he wouldn't have spent both nights dancing with me."

"But he liked me! I know he liked me. . . ." Kayla's voice trails off. She juts her quivering chin at Cinderella. "I can't believe I helped you! Prince robber!"

Betty smiles a seriously evil smile. "Don't get all worked up, Kayla. Cinderella isn't marrying the prince. She couldn't raise the hundred dollars."

"Yes, she could. It's right here." I pull out the envelope with the money. "See? There's enough in here for the apartment plus twenty dollars extra."

"Let's see about this, shall we?" Betty walks over to me. "Tell me something, who paid for the ingredients that Cinderella used to bake the crownies?"

"We bought the ingredients for the second batch at the market," Jonah says.

Betty raises an eyebrow. "What about the first batch?"

"We found the ingredients in the house," I say, my voice shaking.

"So that means you used *my* ingredients for *your* crownies. Without asking my permission. Which, in my book, is stealing. I don't know what kind of laws you have in Smithville, but here in Floom stealing is a crime." She laughs. "Forget the attic. You should see what a jail cell feels like."

"Take twenty dollars." Cinderella says quickly. "Then we'll be even."

"Will we now?" Betty says. "Twenty dollars hardly seems enough for all the ingredients you stole. And what about the paper you used to make the signs? And the ironing board you used as a table? I'd say you owe me, including penalties and interest . . ." She pretends to be hard at thought. "Hmm. How much did you say you made? A hundred and twenty dollars? I'd say you owe me a hundred and thirty." Her mouth twists into an evil smile. "Aw. You don't have that much. Too bad. I guess this means you and your little Smithvillian friends are going to jail."

"Mom, no!" Beatrice yells.

Can it be? Did I have it all wrong? Is Beatrice the nice one and Kayla the bad one?

"If they all go to jail," Beatrice whines, "who's going to do the cooking and the laundry?"

Betty smiles. "Think, Beatrice. Whichever one of you marries the prince will move me and your sister into the palace with you, yes?"

Beatrice nods. "Surely,"

"Then we'll each have our own maid to tend to us — who needs Cinderella?"

My heart pounds. I turn to Farrah. "Can't you stop her? She's being ridiculous!"

Farrah shakes her head. "She's the lady of the house. Cinderella should have asked her permission before taking her things. There's nothing I can do."

"Your choice," Betty says with a grin. "A hundred and thirty dollars — or jail."

I look at Kayla, my eyes pleading. "I know you're mad, but can't you convince them to go easy on us? Remember how crummy you felt for treating Cinderella badly for so long? Haven't you changed at all?"

Kayla's lips quiver but then she takes a deep breath. "Mom," she says finally. "You're being unfair. Cinderella didn't know she was stealing. She lives here, you know. She just assumed it was her stuff, too."

"Well, it wasn't, and now she has to pay," Betty spits out.

I send Kayla another pleading glance. "I know you think Cinderella marrying the prince is unfair," I say. "But the way you treated her since she was twelve is even MORE unfair. You owe it to her to help! You know you do!"

Kayla face falls. "I know, I know. Mom, I'll give you the hundred and thirty dollars, okay? Just don't send Cinderella to jail. She's suffered enough."

"Excuse me," Farrah pipes up, "but that breaks the rules."

Cinderella and I exchange a look. "What rules?" she asks.

Farrah frowns. "The rules about being self-sufficient. If Kayla just gives her mother the money, she'd be rescuing Cinderella. Haven't you been listening? Cinderella has to prove she's self-reliant. That's the whole point."

"See?" Betty says. "Even the skinny fairy woman agrees. I think it's time I called the police."

Wait. "You have a phone?" Can I call home?

"Phone! Crownies! Are you guys just making up words to confuse me?" Beatrice asks.

I guess that's a no.

Wait. Did she say crownie? Oh, oh, oh!

"Farrah," I say slowly, "if Cinderella earns the money to pay back Betty, that would prove she's self-reliant?"

"How can I earn the money?" Cinderella says. "I have no ingredients to make more crownies and no money to buy them, and even if I did, we're almost out of time! The prince's assistant is going to be here any minute!"

I reach into my bag and pull out the one remaining crownie. "You still have one crownie left to sell. Kayla, please, please, please would you be interested in buying this crownie for a hundred and thirty dollars?" I turn to Kayla and hold my breath. Who's she going to side with?

"She would not," Betty snaps.

Kayla's cheeks redden. "Actually, Mom, I would."

"Really?" Jonah asks. "You know it has walnuts, right?"

"I can't believe you'd betray your own mother," Betty snarls at Kayla.

"I'm sorry, Mom. I don't want to betray you. I want to make up the last few years to Cinderella."

Farrah looks at her watch. "Five . . . four . . . three . . . two . . . one! You made it! I'm very impressed."

"Think again, fairy freak," Betty says. "Do you see money in my hand? You do not. Cinderella goes to jail."

"Um, actually?" I say. "Speaking as her lawyer, the

negotiations were completed before the deadline, so I would say she's in the clear. Right, Farrah?"

In response, Farrah raises her wand, points it at Cinderella's foot, and zaps it. There's a puff of sparkle, and before our very eyes, Cinderella's foot shrinks back to its normal pre-marshmallow size.

"I'm healed!" Cinderella says, wriggling her toes. "Thank you, Farrah!"

"As for you two," Farrah says to me and Jonah, "it's time to tell you how to get home."

"Really?" I ask.

"Really," she says, twirling the wand between her fingers. "The portal is actually —"

She's interrupted by a loud knock at the front door.

Jonah rushes to the window. "There's a carriage outside! It must be the prince's assistant!"

"Get her!" I hear.

The next thing I know, Beatrice jumps onto Farrah's back, the wand flies out of Farrah's hand, and Beatrice and Farrah tumble to the ground. The wand goes rolling across the floor.

Betty scoops it up. "Now where were we?"

✳ chapter twenty ✳

Squeak

g ive that back immediately," Farrah commands.

Betty's evil-scary smile returns. "I don't think so. Let's see. Now that I have the power, what shall I do with it?"

"I'm guessing you're going to abuse it," Cinderella says wryly.

Betty swishes toward Cinderella and hurls a zap her way.

There's a burst of yellow sparkle and then Cinderella starts to shrink. She gets smaller and smaller and then even smaller. And turns gray. And grows a tail.

"Cool," Betty says. "I must have pressed the mouse-making button."

Oh. My. Goodness. She turned Cinderella into a mouse. A mouse wearing itty-bitty clothes.

"Stop that," Farrah demands, her hands on her hips.

Betty just laughs and turns to Jonah.

"Don't you dare," I yell as I jump in front of him. Zap! Sparkle!

All I can see is yellow, and then zoom! The room is suddenly increasing in size. I feel sick. It's like I'm on a Tilt-A-Whirl. And then — *plunk*. I'm on my tush, with my legs in the air in front of me.

Except they are not my legs. They are little twig legs. They are gray. And I have a tail.

I'm a mouse.

ARGHHHH!

I look at Jonah.

He's a mouse, too. A baby mouse in a red sweatshirt and jeans. A baby mouse who is currently trying to catch his tail.

"Achoo!" sneezes the Cinderella mouse.

I try to say *bless you*, but instead what comes out is, "Squeak!"

"Hand that wand back to me this instant," Farrah warns, taking a step toward her.

Betty turns the wand on Farrah next. "I don't think so." Zap! Sparkle!

Farrah yelps as she starts to shrink and turn green and scaly.

"A lizard button!" Betty says gleefully. "This thing is fantastic!"

What are we going to do? Farrah's a lizard in a yellow top and black leggings! And we're mice! What if we're stuck like this forever? Even if the Farrah lizard somehow shows us how to get home, we can't go back to Smithville as mice! My parents will never know it's us! They'll catch us with traps and hurt us and not even know it!

There's another knock on the front door. "Is anyone home?" we hear.

"Mom, turn them back into people right now," Kayla demands.

"Sorry, sweetie, I couldn't hear you. Did you say squeak?" And with that she turns her wand on Kayla and zaps her.

This is insane. Betty just turned her own daughter into a mouse. A very *large*, brown mouse with very sharp teeth. Wait a sec. Is she a —

"You're a rat! How fitting," Betty snarls. She smiles and then yells downstairs, "Coming!" She turns to Beatrice. "But first things first. Let's resize those feet." She points the wand at her daughter's left foot and zaps it.

It *resizes* all right. It expands. And expands some more. It expands into the size of a basketball. And then turns orange. It's a pumpkin!

"Mom!" Beatrice shrieks.

"Sorry, sorry. Hold on." Betty pulls out a pair of glasses from her pocket and studies the wand. "Aha! There it is. Reduction button." She zaps her daughter's left foot again and it shrinks back to its original size and color. Then she zaps it once more and it shrinks even smaller. She zaps the right foot next. "That should do it. Grab the slipper, will you, dear?"

"With pleasure," Beatrice says, and then cackles.

"Coming!" Betty calls again, and the mother and daughter hurry downstairs, slamming the attic door behind them.

"Squeeeeeak!" I yell. Which really means, *We have to follow them!*

"Squeak!" say Cinderella and Kayla at the same time.

"Squinx," says my brother gleefully, which I'm assuming is mouse for jinx.

We all scurry to the door. Um. Small problem. We are way too short to reach the handle. Now what?

"Squeak," Jonah says again, and proceeds to try to squeeze himself under the door. Oh, no. What if he gets stuck? But he doesn't. He goes right under. Mice are very squirmy.

I squeeze through to the other side, too. Cinderella goes next. Then Kayla. Then Farrah. I guess rats and lizards are squirmy, too.

We made it! They all follow me as I scamper down the stairs and into the living room.

Betty is standing by the couch, her arms behind her back holding the glass slipper that Farrah fixed. Beatrice is sticking her foot out as the prince's assistant crouches in front of her with the other glass slipper.

And the prince. I did not expect him to be here, too, but the prince is sitting on the love seat looking regal and princely in his very purple robe.

"Squeak!!!!" cries the Kayla rat.

"Thank you so much for the tea," the prince says. "That was very thoughtful of you."

"I'm sure everyone is showering you with treats," says Betty.

The assistant nods. "The last house we were at had these amazing little cake things. They're called crownies, I'm told.

Cinderella's Crownies. They bought them at the market. Have you ever had one?"

"They're quite delicious," the prince says.

Betty grunts. "I've heard they make a lot of crumbs."

Cinderella squeaks.

Wait a sec. The assistant looks familiar. He's skinny and he has a goatee. It's the guy from the coat check! I guess he got promoted. Way to go!

"Time to do the shoe thing," the goatee guy says. He lifts the glass slipper to Beatrice's left foot.

Please don't fit, please don't fit, please don't fit.

It fits.

Crumbs is definitely right.

* chapter twenty-one *

Hickory Dickory

Prince Jordan," goatee guy says, "say hello to your bride."

No, no, no! We have to do something to stop this!

Beatrice slides the right slipper onto her foot and does a little victory dance with her shoulders.

Prince Jordan smiles as he approaches her. "Hello, um — who are you again?"

Beatrice curtsies and then straightens up. "Beatrice."

"You're much taller than I remember," he says, sounding perplexed.

"It's your imagination," Betty says. She's stuck the wand

behind her ear like a pencil. Is that any way to treat a wand? No, it is not.

Kayla-rat scurries up the couch, jumps on her sister's shoulder and tries to bite her.

"Mom, we really need to get an exterminator in here," Beatrice says tossing her sister to the ground.

And *we* need to steal back the wand. I scurry across the room and assess the situation. A couch, a love seat, a fireplace, a chandelier, and a grandfather clock. I need to get at Betty from above if I want to snatch the wand. If I can somehow make it to the chandelier, maybe I can jump on her head? But how will I get to the chandelier? I'm pretty sure mice can't fly.

Still, if fairy tales have taught me anything, they *can* run up a clock. Like in "Hickory Dickory Dock"!

Okay, so technically that's a nursery rhyme, but it's still worth a shot.

I can do this. I scurry over to the ledge at the bottom of the clock and dig right in. This is easier than I thought. I use my itty-bitty nails to claw and climb to the top in just a matter of seconds. Ha! And they say *time* flies.

Except here I am, perched on top of the clock. Now what?

The chandelier is too far away for me to make the jump. What I really need is for Betty to take a few steps backward. Come on, Betty, move it!

Jonah looks up and sees me. "Squeak?" he asks, which I interpret to mean, *What are you doing up there?*

I'd squeak right back at him, but I don't want to draw attention to myself. Instead, I try to use my little mouse-hands, pantomime style, to tell him what to do.

So far I haven't been successful with any of my hand gesturing, but this time we have liftoff. He seems to understand, because the next thing I know, he's bashing himself against Betty's shoe like a bumper car.

She takes a step back. Go, Jonah, go!

Bash!

Step back.

Almost there . . .

Bash!

Except she's getting annoyed. She swings her foot back and — no! — kicks Jonah with the pointy toe of her shoe and sends him flying across the room. He somersaults through the air and lands in the fireplace.

Hey, that's my brother you're kicking around!

"Squeooonah!" I yell, and before I realize what I'm doing, I'm flying, supermouse style, straight for the top of Betty's head.

Plunk.

"What —" Betty says.

Before she figures out what's happening, I grab the wand with my pudgy little mouse-fingers and yank it from behind her ear.

Now the wand and I are on a collision course with the ground.

✳ chapter twenty-two ✳

Kazam

Ohmyohmyohmy!

The floor is coming at me fast and I'm holding on tight to the wand.

We land with a thud and a burst of sparkle.

Yay!

"Yes, we definitely need an exterminator," Betty growls, reaching down for the wand, a terrifying expression on her face.

No, no, no! She is not getting back this wand. I transfer it to my mouth and run, run, run toward lizard-Farrah, who's currently helping mouse-Jonah out of the fireplace. He's covered in ashes, but otherwise fine.

"I'll catch it," goatee guy says, chasing after me.

There's a straight line from me to Farrah. All I have to do is run. Or, maybe scurry is the right word.

"Just step on the thing," Betty says, which chills my spine and sends me running even faster.

But then — whoosh!

My tail! Goatee guy has my tail! He's picking me up by my tail!

My feet are lifting in the air, and I realize I only have one shot. I harness all my energy and give the edge of the wand the strongest shove I can muster, sending it skidding across the room.

"Is that mouse wearing a dress?" goatee guy asks.

Betty is too busy running toward the wand to answer.

I strain my neck to see the wand barrel toward Farrah and the fireplace. And . . . it makes it! She jumps on it!

There's a huge burst of yellow sparkle and Farrah stretches into her normal self.

Goatee guy gasps and drops me, and once again I plummet to the ground. Ouch. I'm getting tired of all this plummeting.

"Farrah, is that you?" Prince Jordan asks.

"Hey, Jordy," Farrah says. "Good to see you again. You're looking well." She holds the wand up in the air and spins around and around and around. A splatter of yellow sparkle flies around the room.

Everything changes at once. I feel like I'm on that Tilt-A-Whirl again and I'm stretching, stretching, stretching until I look down at my legs and realize I'm no longer mouse-Abby.

I'm person-Abby once again.

Yay!

Jonah and Cinderella have morphed back as well.

Yay and yay again!

And then there's the sound of cracking glass.

"OWWW!" Beatrice screams.

Her feet have doubled in size, and the glass slippers have cracked right open because of the pressure.

"This is not the girl I danced with," says the prince. "I fear you're trying to trick me. Our shoe doesn't even fit, and neither does the other one! Come on, Gary, we're leaving."

"No, wait!" Betty exclaims, a wild look in her eye. "I have another daughter you can marry. She's running around here somewhere. . . ."

"Mother, I'm right here," Kayla says, stretching back into her human form.

"Can someone please tell me what's going on?" Prince Jordan demands.

"I'd be happy to," I say. "You're right. Beatrice is not the girl you danced with. Her mother stole Farrah's wand, turned us all into animals, and zapped her daughter's feet so they'd fit in the glass slippers."

"So then who do the shoes belong to?" His gaze falls on Kayla. "Is it you? I *know* you. We talked at the ball, right? You made me laugh."

She hesitates, but then shakes her head. "Yes, I did," she says. "But no." She kicks up her heel. "These tootsies are size nine. No way they're squeezing into those teeny-sized shoes."

Prince Jordan's face falls. "But then who —"

"They're Cinderella's!" Jonah yells, pointing at her.

He turns to her. "You?"

Cinderella nods nervously.

"Let me just repair the shoes with a zap and you'll see for yourself," Farrah says. She waves her wand toward the slippers, enveloping them in a burst of yellow. "There you go. Try them on, dear. You've earned it."

"But — but — but —" Beatrice stutters.

"No buts," I say. "Now please get out of Cinderella's happy ending."

Beatrice lets out a loud *humph*, and then tries to follow her mother, who is slowly backing toward the door.

"Why don't you two hang around for a while?" Farrah says, and sends a sparkle-zap their way.

They instantly shrink into two little birds. Two caged little birds. Two caged little birds in drab gray dresses.

The prince turns to Cinderella. "Hi, again," he says.

"Hi, yourself," she says softly.

"Ready for the shoe test?"

Cinderella sighs and takes a seat on the couch. She kicks off her loafers. "Let's do this."

He picks up the first shoe and it slips perfectly onto her foot. He picks up the second and it does the same.

"Hurray!" we all cheer. Jonah and I high-five.

Farrah grins.

Even Kayla says, "Congratulations. I'm happy for the two of you." But she has a sad look on her face.

The prince takes Cinderella's hand and pulls her to her feet. He crouches on one knee. "Cinderella, will you do me the honor of being my wife?"

Finally! It all worked out! The story can go on as planned! We saved the day!

Cinderella looks at Prince Jordan and then at Kayla and then back at the prince and then back at Kayla and then down at her glass slippers. "Prince Jordan, I'm so sorry, but —" She takes a deep breath. "No."

✳ chapter twenty-three ✳

Huh?

everyone gasps.

Jonah tugs at my arm. "Abby, why did she say no? Isn't she supposed to say yes?"

"I don't know!" I say. I really don't. What happened here?

Cinderella sits back down and pulls off the slippers. "I'm so sorry," she says. "Two days ago, there was nothing I wanted more than to marry you. I wanted you to rescue me. But since the ball, I got to stand on my own two feet and make my own money, and now everything is different. I love making crownies. I want my own place. And I don't really love you . . . not the way Kayla does. You deserve someone who loves you for the right reasons. Everyone does."

We all look at the prince for his reaction. I kind of expect anger. Or bafflement. But what I see instead surprises me.

He looks relieved.

"To be honest," he says, "it was my father who was so taken with you. Not that you're not beautiful. You are. But I really enjoyed the time I spent with . . ." He turns to Kayla. "Excuse me, what's your name again?"

Kayla squeaks. Nope, she's not a rat again, she's just excited. "Kayla," she finally sputters.

He smiles at her. "I was secretly hoping the slipper would fit you, not Cinderella." He looks at Cinderella. "No offense, okay?"

"None taken," she says.

"This is wonderful," Farrah says. "I'm so happy for you three!"

It is a super-happy ending. Different from the original ending, but I like it anyway.

Prince Jordan hesitates. "But . . . I've already made a royal proclamation that whoever fits the slipper will be the new princess. I can't undo that."

No, no, no! They will have this happy ending! "Maybe you can't undo it," I say, "but I can." I pick up both slippers and throw them hard against the brick fireplace, smashing them to smithereens. "Oops."

"Yay!" Jonah cheers. "No more slippers! I guess Kayla can't try them on."

"You do know that I can fix them," Farrah points out.

We all stare at her, holding our collective breath.

She smiles. "Of course, if I do, there's no guarantee they'll be the same size as before."

"In that case," the prince says, "I'm officially declaring the slipper test invalid, since it's so inaccurate." He bends back down on one knee. "Kayla, will you do me the honor of being my bride?"

"Yes," she says as a tear trickles down her cheek.

Hurray!

"Isn't it romantic?" goatee guy says. I notice that he's gazing at Cinderella.

"It is," she answers him with a shy smile.

"I really enjoyed your crownies," he says. "I'm Gary, by the way."

"Thank you. I'm Cinderella"

"I'll have to come by your bakery and get some for myself."

"That would be lovely," she says, and then . . . bats her eyelashes?

Cinderella and Gary the Goatee Guy? Who would have thought?

Farrah puts her arm on my shoulder. "I guess it's time for you and your brother to go home now."

"Yes, please." I say. "Can you tell us where the magic mirror is?"

"Abby!" Jonah says. "Abby, I think —"

"Not now, Jonah," I say. "I'm trying to get us home."

"But, Abby —"

"Jonah, please hold on. Farrah? The mirror?"

Farrah shakes her head. "There is no magic mirror."

"Don't say that." My panic is rising. "Sure, I like it here in Floom, but we need to get home! I'm not even one hundred percent sure what time it is at home."

"Abby," Jonah says a little more forcefully. "I know how we get home."

I turn to him. "You do?"

"Yes."

"How?"

"The fireplace!"

I look at the fireplace and then back at him. "Are you crazy?"

"No! It's true! When I fell into it, I'm pretty sure I heard it hiss."

"No way!" I say.

I turn to Farrah for confirmation that my brother is crazy, but see that she's nodding. "Way?" I ask her.

"Way," she says.

"But how?"

"Fairies can enchant different household objects and appliances. It doesn't always have to be a mirror."

I stare at her, trying to comprehend what she's saying. "Are you telling us that Maryrose is a fairy?"

"Of course she's a fairy! How else could she enchant your basement mirror? Didn't she tell you she's a fairy?"

We shake our heads.

"Oh. Oops. She's very mysterious that Maryrose. So do you guys want to go home or what?"

We both nod.

"Let's do it!" Farrah says. "I have places to be, you know."

"We may want to sweep up the fireplace first," I say. "It's covered in glass."

"I'll do it!" Cinderella calls out.

"Don't worry," Jonah says, going to get the broom. "I've got it."

We're never getting out of here.

When we're ready, we give big good-bye hugs to Cinderella and Kayla and shake hands with Gary the Goatee Guy and Prince Jordan.

"What are you going to do about Betty and Beatrice?" I ask Farrah.

She frowns. "I suppose I'd better turn them back before they peck each other to death. But it's your call, Kayla."

"All right," Kayla says. "Turn them back. But in about an hour or so. You can do it remotely, right? By then Cinderella and I will be long gone. They are definitely not moving to the palace with me." She turns to Cinderella. "You don't mind if I crash at your new digs until the wedding, do you?"

"Of course not," Cinderella says.

"I'll do the cleaning," Kayla says.

"I'll do the cooking," Cinderella says. "Ever since my mouse experience, I'm kind of craving mac and cheese. Or a four-cheese pizza. And cheese and crackers. Pretty much anything with cheese."

"So what do we do?" Jonah asks Farrah. "Should I knock?"

"No need," Farrah says. "We know you're there. Both of you crouch inside and tell me when you're ready."

We wave good-bye and squat in the fireplace. I notice there's a fairy — with wings — carved into the stone. Didn't the magic mirror at Snow's have that, too?

"We're ready!" Jonah says.

There's a burst of yellow sparkle and the next thing I know, we're zoom, zoom, zooming up the chimney.

* chapter twenty-four *

Home Sweet Home

We pop right up the chimney and pop out of our basement mirror.

"Ow," I say. "That hurt. You okay?"

Jonah is already hopping on his feet. "I'm great. That was so much fun! Can we go back?"

"Now?"

"I'm wide awake," he says. "It's only two in the afternoon in Floom."

"On our last trip, one day in fairy tale land turned out to be about one hour at home. So that means it's about two thirty in the morning here. We should probably go to sleep."

But first I turn back to the silent mirror. "Maryrose? Are you there? Can we talk? We'd love to know why you keep sending us into different fairy tales."

No answer.

"Maybe tomorrow," Jonah says.

I roll my eyes. "Why do we keep coming back if she won't even tell us what's going on?"

"Because it's fun," Jonah says. "And she'll tell us eventually. She'll have to."

We hike up the stairs and I peek at the microwave clock. Wait a sec. "It's not two in the morning. It's *six* in the morning."

His eyes bulge. "That was close. Mom and Dad wake up in one hour!"

I don't get it. Last time, every day in fairy tale land was an hour back home. This time we were gone for two and three-quarter days, which is about . . . sixty-six fairy tale hours. It doesn't add up!

"I guess time depends on the story," Jonah says.

"I guess."

"Next time, bring your watch," he says.

"What next time? Did I agree on a next time?"

He nods knowingly. "There will be a next time."

We climb back up the stairs to the top floor and open the door to my parents' room to carefully peek in. *Creak.*

"Shush!" I whisper, but they don't budge.

"Don't worry," Jonah says. "They won't wake up. They're really tired."

"They've been working really hard," I say. I suddenly feel guilty about all the grief I've given them. They just started a new law firm — that's why we moved to Smithville. And starting a new business — is *hard*. I know, because I just helped start one. There are so many details to think about! And running a home is tough, too.

"I guess it's kind of tough to be in their shoes," I say.

"Bed?" Jonah asks.

"Bed," I say, and I close the door. "A real bed, too. Straw on the floor, I will not miss you."

"Good night, Ab," Jonah says.

I give him a tight hug.

Then I step into my room and over to my jewelry box. I want to see Cinderella.

She's there, smiling. But now instead of her poofy platinum dress, she's wearing a poofy baker's hat. And an apron that says CINDERELLA'S CROWNIES.

Aw! Yay, Cinderella!

Snow is standing beside her, still in my lime-green pajamas.

Oh, no! I forgot my polka-dot pajamas in Floom! Oh well. They were ridiculous pajamas anyway. And I guess they belong in Floom, since they're the flag and everything.

I strip off my dress, which is covered in gray soot. I'm about to toss it into the hamper when I realize something.

My hamper is full.

And I'm wide awake.

I have an idea. I pull my overstuffed laundry bag out of the hamper and drag it out the door.

I knock on Jonah's door.

"Yeah?"

"Laundry run," I say, opening it. I take out his bag and drag it all downstairs to the laundry room off the kitchen.

If I can do it by hand in Floom, I can figure out the machine in Smithville.

But how much detergent to use?

I read the directions. Easy, peasy. It's like following a recipe.

Not that I'm agreeing to another adventure or anything, but it's always good to have clean non-wedgie undies ready.

Just in case.

acknowledgements

Thank you, thank you, thank you:

Laura Dail, my super agent who never gave up on (Farrah/Keri) Abby; and Tamar Rydzinski, the queen of foreign rights.

My excellent editors, Aimee Friedman and AnnMarie Anderson, and the rest of the Scholastic team: Abby McAden, Becky Shapiro, Janet Robbins, Allison Singer, Bess Braswell, Emily Sharpe, Lizette Serrano, Emily Heddleson, Candace Greene, Becky Amsel, and David Levithan.

Joel Gotler and Brian Lipson for all their hard work in Hollywood.

First readers and editors Elissa Ambrose, Courtney Sheinmel, and Emily Jenkins. (Rock stars, all three of you.)

Also, Louisa Weiss, Leslie Margolis, and Aviva Mlynowski, for their awesome notes.

Special callout to Tori, Carly, and Carol Adams for their support and enthusiasm. Yay, Torly Kid!

Targia Clarke for taking such good care of my family.

Also thanks to: Larry Mlynowski, Jess Braun, Adele Griffin, Jess Rothenberg, Julia DeVillers, Lauren Myracle, Joanna Philbin,

Emily Bender, Alison Pace, John & Vickie Swidler, Robert Ambrose, Jen Dalven, Gary Swidler, Darren Swidler, Ryan and Jack Swidler, Shari and Heather Endleman, the Steins, the Mittlemans, Bonnie Altro, Farrin Jacobs, Robin Wasserman, Tara Altebrando, Meg Cabot, Ally Carter, Maryrose Wood, Jennifer Barnes, Alan Gratz, Sara Zarr, Maggie Marr, Susane Colasanti, Elizabeth Eulberg, and Jen Calonita.

Thanks and love to my husband (also my tech support, life manager, and Prince Charming), Todd. Extra love and kisses to my sweet little Chloe, who always wants just one more story.

DON'T MISS ABBY AND JONAH'S NEXT ADVENTURE:

Whatever After #3
SINK or SWIM

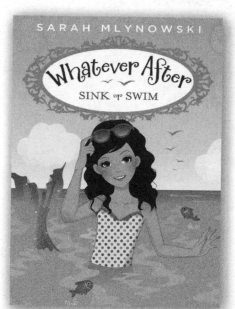

This time, the siblings end up in the story of the Little Mermaid! What kind of antics will they get up to under the sea?